CULTURAL GAP

Elizabeth Fraser

Elizabeth Fraser

ATHENA PRESS
LONDON

ISBN 1 84401 511 4

First Published 2005 by
ATHENA PRESS
Queen's House, 2 Holly Road
Twickenham TW1 4EG
United Kingdom

Printed for Athena Press

Chapter One

'A toast to Fiona,' enthused Isobel.

They all raised their glasses and joined in.

'Happy birthday, Fiona. Many happy returns of the day!'

Isobel had organised the small family gathering to celebrate Fiona's thirty-second birthday.

At thirty-two, Fiona thought to herself, birthdays aren't particularly significant any more. Not like when I was a child, when, like Christmas, they used to be eagerly looked forward to. They seemed to possess some magical quality. It wasn't just the presents to be looked forward to, though that had played a significant part in the anticipation, there was that extra year to be added onto my age. That meant I was getting bigger and somehow that was all-important.

Fiona remembered when she had been about seven, enviously looking at the big girls in their final year at primary school. They were eleven years old and how big, important, knowledgeable and self-assured they had seemed to be.

When I'm eleven, thought Fiona at that time, I'll be big like that and ready to go on to the academy. I'll be important then and not a child any more.

Funnily enough, when she had reached that all-important age of eleven and had moved on to the academy at twelve, she found that that magic age she'd grasped at eluded her and moved further on up the scale to, first fifteen, when she would be old enough to leave school, then to eighteen, when she would have finished her Highers, then on to twenty-one, when she would be considered a 'real adult'. Now, she was beginning to conclude that, if she wasn't careful, she could constantly shift the 'goal posts' and never ever attain an age when she would consider herself grown-up, knowledgeable or important! It seemed to her that the more she learned the more there was she didn't know.

These then, were Fiona's innermost thoughts as she turned thirty-two.

She was drinking her whisky and lemonade slowly. Dad, Stanley and Bruce were drinking beer, but they had all had a nip of whisky to toast her. Mum was sipping sherry and Isobel, like Fiona, had whisky and lemonade.

'Sorry I didn't have time to bake a birthday cake today for you. I was sure you wouldn't mind though,' said Isobel apologetically.

'She's a bit big for birthday cakes now,' interrupted Bruce jokingly, 'but I wouldn't have minded a nice slice of your chocolate cake, Isobel. Now that you are big enough, Fee, when are you going to marry me?' Bruce said in his usual jovial, teasing manner.

'Fee' was the nickname the family often used for Fiona.

'That'll be the day. I'm not scraping the bottom of the barrel yet you know!' Fiona retorted impudently.

They all laughed as they continued to drink and chat. The three men, as usual, were discussing work, whilst Mum was speaking to Isobel about baby Ian's progress. Ian was currently the most important family member, being the first grandchild, born only seven months ago to Fiona's brother, Stanley, and his wife, Isobel.

For as long as Fiona could remember she'd been mercilessly teased and tormented by her brother, Stanley, and his school friend, Bruce. They were both four years older than her. They'd always acted the big boys and objected to trailing Fiona along with them – a mere girl – in their younger days when that four-year gap between them seemed enormous. Nowadays, of course, the age gap between them was insignificant, but they both still delighted in tormenting her at every opportunity. Fiona knew that they only did it out of devilment and she accepted their taunting with much good humour.

'Can you babysit tomorrow to let us go to the pictures?' Isobel asked Fiona. 'I can't ask Mother because Friday is her whist night.'

'Of course I can. What time do you want me round?'

'Come straight from school if you like and have tea with us.'

'That's fine. I can help put Ian to bed as well. Do you hear that, Mum, I'll be coming straight round here from school tomorrow night to let Stanley and Isobel go to the pictures, so I'll be late. Don't bother waiting up for me.'

Mum nodded agreement.

The evening passed quickly. It was a pleasant birthday, Fiona thought to herself as she lay in bed that night. It hadn't been celebrated in grand style, but it hadn't slipped past unnoticed either. After all, it was a weekday and added to that, thirty-two wasn't a particularly significant age. She fell asleep quite contented that night.

Next day was Friday and she went straight round to her sister-in-law's house as soon as school closed. She'd been teaching at the Seafield Primary School now for four years. She taught the seven-year-olds and she enjoyed her work there with the children. Living in such a small community she had the advantage of knowing the families of most of her pupils. She felt that helped her understand her pupils better, particularly when any of them showed difficult behavioural patterns. Often she would have a background of family events and relationships which could go a long way to explaining that child's problem. Fortunately, she had few problem children to teach as the more difficult problems usually manifested themselves at older ages. At seven, most of her pupils were happy, loving children, still displaying an eagerness to learn. They were young and innocent and she loved them for these qualities.

Fiona was lucky to have secured the post at Seafield School when Miss MacLeod had retired. Fiona herself had attended the very same school as a child and so had her brother, Stanley, before they both moved to the academy, after the eleven-plus examination. The school was in walking distance, about ten minutes from her parents' house. Stanley and Isobel lived in the next street, so their house was also near the school.

Just think, thought Fiona, little Ian will be going to school in four years' time. I wonder if I'll still be there when he's old enough to be one of my pupils?

Isobel had just returned home from the shops when Fiona arrived, so Ian was still strapped into his high pram. He could easily sit up on his own now and enjoyed his pram outings. The coach-built Marmet pram had been a present from Fiona's parents and Ian could now sit up and see all the shops and people passing from his vantage point. A pram outing was a sure way of pacifying him if he was feeling on the grizzly side. He wasn't too happy to sit in the pram though if it was stationary. He was at that awkward age when his immobility frustrated him. He wanted to be on the move. Fiona was only too happy to amuse him while Isobel put away her shopping and started to prepare tea.

Fiona and Isobel were good friends and spent a lot of time together. They were very comfortable with each other. Fiona knew that Mum was inclined to interfere with Isobel's life and more particularly now since the arrival of Ian. Many a mother likes to think she can look after her son better than a wife can; and what grandmother can resist the temptation of recounting 'how it was done in her day'. Isobel was able to cope astonishingly well with Mum's interference. She seemed to have a surplus of tact and patience. Fiona and Isobel would often laugh about incidents together. Isobel had more diplomacy with Mum than Fiona had, but Fiona had a tendency to let her mother dominate her as an easy option to confrontation.

Isobel, like Fiona, had been born and brought up in the small town and her father, as well as Fiona's father, was involved in the fishing industry. In fact the town was almost entirely dependent on fishing, and like most of the northeast Scottish fishing settlements, they were close-knit communities. Intermarriage amongst the fishing families was common, indeed encouraged. Marriage outside the community was tantamount to marrying a foreigner!

Fishing in the North Sea provided a living for most of these coastal towns and villages and very few lads had their sights set on anything other than going to sea at the first opportunity. Fiona's father ran his own small mobile fish shop from a van. He did daily rounds to the local farming communities and inland towns and villages. When Fiona was small she was sometimes allowed to accompany him on his rounds. This was normally during the school summer holidays. When he stopped, Fiona would get the job of ringing his hand bell, announcing their presence. Then the women would come out with their plates and form a group to see what fish was for sale and make their purchases. Occasionally Fiona would get a sixpence from one of the women for an ice-cream slider. That would make the outing twice as enjoyable.

Fiona's father, Archie Murray, was up early in the morning to attend the fish auction held in the wooden sheds down by the pier. Once he had bought what stock he needed for his van, he called round to the smoking sheds to collect smoked herrings. After that it was home for his breakfast before setting off for the day on his rounds. Fiona seldom went to the fish market with him because it was too early for her. She had been, but the market was a cold, windy place, bustling with noise as the auctioneer quickly sold off the wooden crates of fish which had been landed the previous evening. The floors were perpetually wet with cold water from hosing down the concrete slabs. The fishermen were a hardy group. Their weather-beaten faces gave an indication of the years of exposure to the cold, wet conditions and stormy elements they were accustomed to working in. They aged early and seemed to be 'old' for most of their lives. All of them had experienced tragedy in their lifetimes and yet the sea was their life and fortune as well as their enemy. On the occasions when trawlers were lost at sea, the hands on board were usually related and a family could lose fathers, brothers, sons and friends together. The North Sea could be an unpredictable, treacherous stretch of water to sail. The trawlers were usually owned and crewed by families from this town. Stanley owned a share of a trawler in partnership with his friend, Bruce, Bruce's father and two others. Isobel's father and her two brothers were shareholders of another trawler. So Isobel's husband, Stanley, her father and her two brothers were all at sea.

Isobel often wondered if little Ian would go to sea as soon as he could. Boats and the sea have an excitement surrounding them for most boys and men. Think how many of the wealthy are attracted to the sea for leisure; the fascination of sailing holds a great attraction for many men, even those not brought up in a seafaring environment. That same attraction seems to surround steam trains, racing cars and aeroplanes. Maybe the dangers and unpredictability involved satisfy the need for excitement and that's what draws some to the dangerous occupation of fishing.

Whatever it is about the sea, however cruel it is, Fiona often thought, I still love it. How she had missed it when she'd spent time away from home. There was something therapeutic about being able to walk along stretches of wet sand at low tide and to gaze into the grey, angry, white-topped waves, relentlessly beating onto the shore. There was something that gave Fiona a feeling of permanence when she watched the waves and their continuous motion.

It must have always looked like this, she would think. The town changes; people change; everything and everybody apparently change; but the sea remains exactly the same.

She remembered the sea looked the same when she was a child playing carefree in the dunes and on the seashore with her friends. She expected it would look like this in hundreds of years' time. The sea drew Fiona back to it like a magnet. She always wanted to live within reach of the sea. She'd met people who had never seen the sea. She felt a sadness for them because they had missed something which was so fundamental to her life.

'What do you want for your tea?' Isobel asked.

'What's Stanley having?'

'Black pudding, egg and chips.'

'Egg and chips will do me fine. I don't want any black pudding though. I'll peel the potatoes for you if you like.'

Fiona hadn't eaten black pudding since she found out that blood was one of the ingredients. Funny how the mind can condition one's eating habits.

'What time will Stanley be home?'

'He said round about six. They're busy getting the *Endeavour* ready for Monday's start. They're setting out very early as usual.'

The *Endeavour* was their trawler's name. The boats never fished on Sundays, but they often sailed soon after midnight.

Stanley got home just before six, as good as his word. Isobel had already fed Ian.

'No time for games tonight, my lad,' he said to Ian, who was expecting his father's nightly attention. 'We're off to the pictures and Auntie Fiona's in charge of you.' He then turned to his sister.

'Keep him up as long as you can, Fee, so that he'll maybe sleep in until eight in the morning, so we can have a long-lie.'

'I'll see what I can do.'

Fiona was enjoying herself playing with Ian when Mum called round on her way to the weekly whist drive at the church hall. She left a tin with some shortbread and fruit cake that she'd baked for Isobel. It was Mum's turn to take the eats for the other three women playing at the same whist table. The ladies took it in turns to bring along sandwiches and snacks for tea after the end of the whist drive. Mum enjoyed the whist drives for their social contact with the other local women. Few men attended these meetings, preferring instead to seek their own male company at the local bars. Women didn't go to the local bars. They were for the men only. Fiona wondered why this should still be so in many places in Scotland, whilst in England it was perfectly acceptable for women to accompany their men to the locals.

Ian was starting to show signs of sleepiness when Bruce turned up. He took over with some rough play, which livened Ian up considerably.

'Stanley and Isobel are off to the pictures tonight,' Fiona reminded Bruce.

'I know that. Didn't Stanley tell you I'd be round?'

'No, he didn't. I suppose he forgot.'

'Well, I wanted to see you on your own and I knew you'd be babysitting tonight.'

'Oh, what did you want?'

'Well, can we put this chap to bed first?'

'OK, I'll get him off upstairs. I think he's ready anyway.'

Fiona took Ian upstairs and tucked him in with a bottle of Ribena and waited outside the bedroom door for a while to make sure he was going to settle, and then she went downstairs to see what Bruce wanted.

'I wouldn't say no to a cup of tea.'

'Fine, I'll go and put the kettle on. Mum's just been round with some baking for Isobel. Do you want some cake as well?'

Bruce followed Fiona into the kitchen and opened the lid of the tin Mrs Murray had left on the table.

'I'll have a bit of the fruit cake. Do you want a bit as well?'

'No, thanks. I can get some at home. Better leave what's left for Isobel and Stanley.'

They took their tea through to the living room and sat on the couch in front of the fire. It wasn't a cold night for early June, but cool enough to still need the fire on in the evening.

'Let's get married, Fee,' Bruce suddenly said.

'You're joking, aren't you?' This had naturally taken Fiona off guard.

'No, I'm not. I know this isn't the right way to do this, but I'm not too good with words and I've been wanting to ask you for over a year now and I've never really found the right chance or had enough courage to ask you.'

'What do you want to marry me for anyway?'

'The usual reason folk get married. I guess, because I love you. What do you think of the idea? Surely all the time you've been home and we've been making up a foursome with Stan and Isobel, it must have dawned on you that you're the only person I'd want to marry? You don't go out with anybody else either do you?'

'No, you're right. You're the only person I go out with, but I hadn't really considered getting married. I've been quite contented with my life the way it is. I don't think it would be right to marry you, it wouldn't really be fair to you.'

'Well, that's a bit of an odd answer. Maybe you don't love me, is that it?'

'No, of course not. You know I love you, but marriage is a different ball park altogether.'

'Well, can you give me one good reason why you don't want to get married? You say you do love me, so that's obviously not the problem.'

Fiona looked at him and then burst into tears. This certainly took Bruce by surprise as he hadn't expected such a reaction.

'Yes, of course I love you in my own peculiar way. You've always been around. All my life we've known each other, but I can't marry you or anybody else, I just can't,' she sobbed.

'Come, come now, Fee, come and sit beside me and tell me what's upsetting you and why you're crying.'

She moved over beside him on the couch and he put his arm round her shoulder and lightly kissed her cheekbone.

'Come, let's talk about this. What's making you so unhappy? What's the problem? Surely we can discuss it? Don't tell me that when you were out in Africa one of those witchdoctors you've told us about put a curse on you?' he said jokingly.

'Oh, Bruce, it's not that at all, but there's so much about me you don't know and I don't deserve you.'

'What's all this about, Fee? I've known you since you were little. Surely you're not going to tell me you're queer, or something like that?'

Again, he was speaking to her in a light-hearted, half-joking way and at the same time squeezing her towards him.

'I'll tell you what. Drink your tea and let's stop crying. Come and tell me what's the matter. Have I upset you, is that it?'

Fiona shook her head and sobbed, 'No, no, it's nothing to do with you. No, you haven't upset me. It's all my fault and I'm so ashamed and sorry.'

After a few minutes, they both drank their tea silently, then Fiona took a deep breath and composed herself.

'Don't you want to tell me what's wrong? I'm sure what's upsetting you can't be as bad as all that?'

'Oh, Bruce, if I tell you, will you promise me that you won't tell anybody else? Please, it's important that it's a secret.'

'Of course I won't tell anybody. You should know me better than that by now.'

'When I tell you, you might change your mind about me and I wouldn't blame you for that.'

'Why don't you try me then? You're not in any kind of trouble, are you?'

'No, not really. It's just that I've had this cooped up inside me and I've had nobody to talk to about it. You know what Mum is like. I've never been able to talk to her about it. She only knows half the story anyway and even the half she does know is treated as a closed book as far as she's concerned. Mum conveniently blots out of her mind what she doesn't like or doesn't approve of, pretending it never existed in the first place. You can't reason with her. She's like everybody here, so narrow-minded and straight-laced.'

'Oh, really, Fee. You know that's not all true. She practically worships the ground you and Stanley walk on.'

'Yes, yes, I know that. I don't mean to criticise her intentions at all, she just wants me to conform and she feels I let her down, disgraced her. She never approved of me leaving home.'

'But that was only because she missed you. You know how happy she's been all these years since you've been back home.'

By this time Fiona was starting to feel much better and said, 'I'm sorry Bruce. I feel such a twit crying on you like that.'

He squeezed her shoulder again and drew her close to his chest and said, 'Tell me now, see if I don't understand. You're probably blowing things out of all proportion. You've got plenty of time, Stan and Isobel won't be home for ages yet.'

'It's a long story though.'

'It'll be our secret, I promise. Then we'll see.'

'You remember when I was out teaching in West Africa when I left teacher training? Well, that was only part of the story. You see I was actually married against Mum's wishes and she sort of disowned me all that time and now she conveniently pretends it never happened. She forbade Dad and Stanley to ever mention it outside the house, so you see nobody here knows.'

'Yes, I remember there was bad feeling when you were away and I know there was a long time when you didn't seem to write to each other often, but I'd no idea what the problem was. I always imagined it was a case of you not keeping in touch and her not really approving of you working so far away from home. She never said very much about it at the time and she always made short of any conversation when your name was brought up. I do remember though when she knew you were coming home how excited she was. Are you still married? Is that the problem?'

'No, I'm divorced now. It's all finished and tidied up long ago.'

'Tell me what happened. It'll do you good to talk about it.'

Chapter Two

Fiona had gone from the academy to teacher training in Nottingham. Her mother hadn't been particularly happy about her going so far away when there were plenty of good colleges so much nearer to home. Nevertheless, Fiona argued that wherever she was studying she would be leaving home and so it was that, when she was eighteen, she left to study for a B.Ed. degree at college in Nottingham.

Her undergraduate years were happy and although she was the only Scottish girl in her year, nearly all her classmates were also living away from home. Each vacation she returned home.

Initially she was in residence, but eventually she moved out to share a house with three other girls from her year. Judith came from Bristol. Her subject was English, the same as Fiona. Sue's subject was Music and she came from Dover and the fourth friend was Margaret from Sunderland and she was a History undergraduate. The four girls lived together for two years in a self-contained part of a large old house in The Park, off Derby Road in Nottingham.

They shared cooking, housework and expenses and on the whole were very good friends. Fiona and Judith were perhaps closest, because they shared the same lectures and timetable at college.

In the final year of the B.Ed. course, Fiona was placed at a junior school in Netherfield, very close to Nottingham, for her final teaching practice assignment. It was during this time that she met Wil.

Travelling to and from school daily meant two bus journeys, with a change in the centre of town. She hadn't noticed him at first, but on a few occasions he got off the bus at the same stop as she always did on Derby Road. He was always downstairs whereas she preferred to travel on the upper deck. She didn't smoke, but she liked the extra view from the top of the bus. She could see over the garden hedges and look into gardens.

One Thursday evening in winter on her way home it was wet, dark and generally cold and miserable. She got off the bus just in front of him and stood under the bus shelter.

He smiled hesitantly at her and said, 'Don't you want to share my umbrella with me? You'll get wet otherwise.'

'Thanks very much, but I haven't got very far to go from here and I'll just make a dash for it. I'm only going as far as The Park.'

'Tell you what, I'll walk down to the entrance of The Park with you and then you can run from there. I'm going that way. I'm going to visit a friend who lives down Seely Road. Are you a student?'

'Yes, but I'm in my final year. I'm on teaching practice at the moment. I think I've seen you on the bus before.'

'That's quite possible, I visit here often. A friend I work with lives in a house down on Seely Road. It's near the school at the bottom of the street.'

'Yes, I know that school on the corner of Douglas Road and Ilkeston Road. Where do you live then?'

'Me? Oh, I live at the General. I live in there.'

'The General Hospital?'

'Yes, that's it. By the way, my name's Wil. What's yours?'

'Oh, I'm Fiona. Pleased to meet you and thanks for the half of your umbrella.'

'Glad to be of help. Perhaps we'll meet again on another rainy night,' Wil laughed.

'This should teach me to always carry my umbrella. I should know there's always a good chance of it raining by now.'

With that they parted, each to go in their separate directions. She ran off down the dark tree-lined pavement and turned right into Pelham Crescent leading to the cul-de-sac where she lived.

After that Wil started to join Fiona upstairs on the bus whenever he was visiting his friend and they chatted about themselves.

Soon she found out that he was a doctor at the General Hospital and he was thirty-two and he came from the small West African country of Sierra Leone. He had been sent to school in England when he was fifteen and had graduated from medical school in Edinburgh and for the past two years had been working in Nottingham.

Their relationship moved fast over the next couple of months. First of all they would meet for coffee in town before taking the bus together. Soon they were constant companions, spending as much time together as possible between Fiona's lectures, assignments and revision and Wil's hospital shifts. Fiona was due to sit her finals in June and with her teaching practice now ending she had to concentrate on her revision.

By May of that year she had known Wil for only three months, but she was completely besotted with him. To describe her as being happy would have been an understatement. She felt as though her feet were no longer touching the ground. Life took on a different dimension; she felt as though she was literally floating through life. Her senses were more acute, colours were brighter; everything around gave her pleasure. She was happy beyond the point she'd ever been before. Problems were trivial; she had enough enthusiasm and energy to cope with any and all of life's weary problems, should there be any.

They spent time together, enjoying each other's company. During that month of May they visited parks like the Arboretum, and Wollaton, and the forests and woodlands around Nottingham. Fiona was aware of the beauty of the grass, the plants and the flowers all around. Wil literally swept her off her feet!

They spent time at Wil's flat and Fiona willingly submitted to her strong sexual feelings. They soon became lovers. It's what they both wanted. She'd never dreamt being in love could heighten her sexual feelings and desires so much. Sex together seemed so right for both of them and because they were so much in love, there was no thought given to not indulging their strong desires for each other. After all, what was there to wait for?

Fiona lived from day to day and she gave little thought to the future. Her main considerations were to see Wil and to pass the examinations in June. This was the most wonderful time she'd ever experienced in the whole of her twenty-two years. They were totally engrossed with each other. She thought that life had never been better.

Judith had met Wil on a few occasions, even though Sue and Margaret hadn't. Judith had of course discussed Fiona's romance with them and between them they decided that they perhaps ought to determine how serious the relationship was getting.

One Thursday in late May when the four of them were all at home revising for the forthcoming finals, Margaret asked, 'When are you going to introduce Sue and me to your Wil?'

'Any time you like. It's just that you've never been around to meet him so far.'

'When you seeing him again?'

'It'll be Sunday now as he's on duty tomorrow and Saturday.'

'I bet you'll miss him when you go home after the exams are finished. You've been spending all your spare time with him lately. Are you still going back home to look for a job, or what's going to happen now? You won't be able to carry on a long-distance romance for very long from the north of Scotland, will you? It will soon fizzle out.'

The three girls looked at Fiona for her reply.

'Actually, I've not really thought too much about what to do once the exams are over, but I know already that I want Wil more than anything else. I'll perhaps have to start applying for jobs locally so I won't have to leave him.'

'Have you told your mum that you're going out with a black chap yet?' asked Sue tentatively.

'No, not yet. I thought I'd tell them at home when I go in July. I'm sure they'll be OK about it though.'

'Do you really think they'll approve?' Sue went on, emphasising the word 'really'. 'I don't think my parents would be all that pleased if I announced I was courting somebody black. How would your folks look at it?' Sue looked to Judith and Margaret.

That finished the studying for the time being and the four of them discussed the subject over supper. The three girls tactfully tried to tell Fiona what they expected her to be up against at home by continuing a serious relationship with Wil. They tried to tell her what antagonism she could expect and that they all thought that the relationship could lead to nothing short of disaster and heartbreak for her. They tried to treat the matter tactfully, but went straight to the heart of the matter.

'You know,' Judith added, 'people in academic circles, like those we are involved with, are more liberated thinkers than the "ordinary populace". They can accept change more easily. They are more radical with their thinking and acceptance of new and out-of-the-ordinary situations. You'll experience a lot of unpleasantness and resistance to your relationship in the real world. It could even affect your chances of getting a job. Maybe in Wil's circle of friends and your college friends, they'll be willing to accept a black man with a white wife, but I don't think many people will be so tolerant.'

'Who said anything about getting married?'

'Well, if it's only a good friendship, fair enough – then there's no problem,' added Sue. 'It's just if it becomes serious, then you could be faced with problems. When it comes down to the nitty-gritty, so-called liberal thinkers can accept mixed relationships, provided it's not on their own doorstep. Only then do you find out that open-minded parents are suddenly just as narrow-minded as mine would be if I took home a black boyfriend.'

Fiona was slightly miffed at this sudden attack of well-meant advice from the girls and confidently announced, 'I'd really not given the future too much thought, but I do expect that when my parents realise how happy I am with Wil and it's what I want, there won't be a problem.'

Tactfully, the three of them started to back away from the subject and agreed with Fiona that perhaps her parents would be understanding. The more pressing revision then overtook their energy and time.

It was true that Fiona hadn't given any thought to where their relationship was going. She'd been taking each day as it came, perhaps expecting life to continue exactly like it was. She was so happy, she didn't want to think further ahead. The chat with the girls though had a dramatic impact on Fiona and she realised that she didn't want to be without Wil ever again. He made her so happy. He was everything to her and surely her parents couldn't object to him. After all he was well educated, handsome, polite and popular and he had a good job. Why would Archie and Jessie Murray, Fiona's parents, not accept Wil?

True, she'd have to sort out the problem of a job soon. It had always been assumed that once she'd got her teaching degree, she'd go back home and teach locally. But Wil now made that an impossible thought. She couldn't leave him now. It would be like committing suicide – she'd sooner die than be parted from him now. She'd just have to get a job in Nottingham, that's all there was to it. Of course Mum would be disappointed she wasn't coming back to stay at home, but she'd understand eventually.

That night Fiona felt pleased that she'd sorted out what she must do. She'd better have a serious talk with Wil on Sunday and outline her future plans with him.

Everything's going so well for me, she thought to herself as she lay in bed that night. Everything will fall into place nicely. Lucky for me it was raining that night I got off the bus back in February and I met Wil.

It was late on the Sunday morning when she got round to Wil's flat. He'd had a busy night and had only come off duty at seven that morning, so he was still in bed. She joined him in bed after making coffee for both of them. They lay together and made love three times before becoming exhausted.

'That made up for not seeing you for five whole days,' Wil whispered to her.

She was so contented, she could spend all day in bed with him. The touch of his skin made her body throb with desire. She couldn't get close enough to him. She wanted to feel him inside her more than anything else she ever wanted before. He was a gentle lover and he kissed her repeatedly. She wanted time to stand still so that they would always be so much in love and so close as this for ever.

'You know I'll be going home next month, don't you, when I've sat my exams? Will you miss me? Tell me, how much you'll miss me when I'm gone,' she teased.

'You can't go. I can't do without you. You must know how much I love you and how much you mean to me by now?'

'I won't be away too long. We've got the house until the end of August then a post-grad chap from Civil Engineering is taking the place over. I'll have to get sorted out with a job and new accommodation. Before I met you I was going back home for good, but now I've decided to get a job here to be near to you.'

'Why don't we get somewhere together? When did you say you've to be out of The Park?'

'The end of August.'

'We could get somewhere from September and I'll move out of the accommodation at the hospital. That way we can be together nearly all our spare time.'

Things were working out even better than Fiona could have expected. Everything was so simple. This was the answer. They would both be working and they could find somewhere to rent and move in together. Life would be just perfect...

Fiona sat her finals in early June, said a tearful goodbye to Wil and set off home on the overnight train north to Scotland. She intended to be at home for four or five weeks, then return to Nottingham in mid-July to look for a placement in a junior school to start teaching at the beginning of the new school year in September. The school at Netherfield where she had done her final teaching practice had wanted her to work there, but at that time she still intended to look for a teaching post at home. She could contact the headmaster there to see if that post was still vacant.

The Murray family were pleased to have their daughter back home again and even brother Stanley welcomed her. She hadn't been home since the Christmas vacation, and only then for ten days. At Easter she was too preoccupied with Wil and her finals revision to journey north.

The first couple of days passed quickly. The stone-built house which had always been home to Fiona was kept abuzz with visitors, friends, neighbours and relations popped round to say hello to Fiona. She was also busy acquainting herself with her surroundings again, though little had changed. Everything and everybody was just the same as they were at Christmas time, only it was summertime and the weather was better and the daylight hours longer. It wasn't a hot summer, but the weather was mild and comfortable and the evenings were light until about eleven o'clock. How Fiona loved the long summer evenings. Dusk came later by nearly an hour than it did in Nottingham. If only Wil were there to share everything with her. She decided she'd have to tell her parents her future plans, but somehow she couldn't find the right opening to lead into the subject.

On Saturday, Dad was pottering around with the engine of his van and Stanley was giving him the benefit of his expertise. In reality, Dad knew so much more about the van engine. What Stanley knew he had learned from Dad, but Dad was too patient and listened attentively to Stanley's advice. The two of them got on well together and their work in the fishing industry gave them an added mutual interest. They didn't work on Saturdays, but they always had some job in line for that day. Nobody worked on Sundays in the town. Sunday was laid aside for the church and this was still very much adhered to. No boats went to sea to fish on Sundays.

Dad would often go down to the harbour on Saturdays and help Stanley and Bruce on their vessel, *Endeavour*. Otherwise he would just hang around the harbour passing the time of day with some of the other fishermen. There was always someone around to exchange news with over the week's fishing catch, or simply discuss the weather.

That Saturday Fiona helped Mum with shopping and lunch. She had gone down to the corner shop for chips while Mum fried fish. The family sat down together around the kitchen table. They always ate as a family in the kitchen. The dining room was reserved for when visitors came. When that happened the best dishes, cutlery and linen were brought out from the sideboard for the occasion.

'Do you want to come with us to the dance at the Fisherman's Hall tonight?' Stanley asked Fiona.

'That's a good idea,' Mum replied. Mum was good at organising and thinking for them. 'It'll be nice to see the two of you going out together.'

'I don't know if I can be bothered,' was Fiona's unenthusiastic response.

'We can call in at the Stotfield first and have a drink if you like?'

'What time are you going out?'

'Och, about half past seven or eight o'clock I expect.'

'Who's all going?'

'Just the usual crowd of us and some of the girls. The usual Saturday crowd. We usually all meet up in the lounge before going on to the dance.'

'Well, OK then,' Fiona conceded. She knew it would please her mother. 'I'll come down to the Stotfield with you and I'll think about the dance, but you'll have to put a shirt and tie on. I'm not going out with you if you wear a polo neck.' The young fishermen were easily distinguishable when out and about. They had a great affinity to wearing polo-necked sweaters with their suits.

Mum was obviously delighted that they were arranging to go out together. Fiona knew that she wouldn't approve of her going out drinking. Only common girls frequented pubs as far as Mum was concerned, but the lounge at the Stotfield was reasonably acceptable, provided she was accompanied by Stanley.

Off the two of them set that evening. Dad would go down to one of the bars near the harbour later on, for a drink before closing time at nine-thirty. Mum would be busy knitting and listening to the Saturday night story on the radio. She said it was the final episode and she didn't want to miss it.

The lounge was about half-full when they got there so it was easy to get seats and a table in a corner together. When the waitress brought their drinks Stanley toasted Fiona with, 'Cheers, here's hoping we'll get lucky tonight!'

'You speak for yourself, I'm not looking to get off with anybody.'

'Oh, why not? You lined up already, are you?'

'You could say that I suppose.'

'We haven't heard anything about this. You keeping it secret? What's his name? Is it the real thing? You can't get hitched before I do, you know. I'm older than you and I've got to be the first to go.'

Of course, Stanley was teasing Fiona now.

'If you have to know, it's dead serious. Actually he's a doctor,' Fiona said rather arrogantly. She knew that would set Stanley back a bit. 'And his name's Wil.'

'Well, well, Wil… Wil what?'

'Sankoli.'

'What? What kind of a name's that for goodness sake?'

'It's Wilberforce Sankoli, but Wil for short. He's a Sierra Leonean.'

'You mean he's Spanish?'

'No, stupid. Sierra Leone is in West Africa, not Spain.'

Stanley froze in his seat and stared at Fiona. He was silent for all of five seconds, though it seemed much longer at the time. He was completely still, almost comatose and even his eyes didn't move. Fiona could almost hear his brain ticking over and thoughts rushing through his mind.

When he caught his breath he gasped, 'Jesus Christ, Fee, you're not telling me you're going with a golliwog, are you?'

'Don't be obscene. I didn't expect you to be racist.'

'I'm not racist silly, but what about Mum? Boy, do I want to see her face when you tell her. She'd enough to say about Sheila MacDonald from Dunbar Street when she ran off with yon Greek chap. Do you remember that?'

Then, as if stuck for anything else to say he started to laugh and said, 'Well, well, well,' excitedly.

Fiona's defensive mechanism started to move into top gear and she started to justify Wil to her brother. 'What's wrong with somebody from another country? He's just the same as you and me. Why should Mum object? She'll understand when I've told her, you wait and see.'

'Fee, don't you see? He's black and he's foreign. Mum will never come to terms with that. I doubt if she's ever seen anybody black. You should know Mum by now. Remember how she went on and on about Sheila's Greek chap and he was just a bit dingy coloured, not all black. An Englishman would be difficult enough for her to accept but a complete foreigner's another matter altogether.'

Just then a group of Stanley's friends approached them, and Fiona quickly whispered, 'Don't say anything at the moment, Stan, will you, not to the lads or anybody?' It was more a plea than a question.

'No, no, of course I won't say anything. When are you going to tell Mum anyway?'

Fiona didn't have a chance to reply because Stanley's three friends and the two girls with them were already drawing up chairs round the table and deciding what to order and asking Fiona and Stanley what they were drinking. By the time the bar was due to close at half past nine, their group had grown to about a dozen and they then all made their way to the dance hall. It was nearly midnight when they got home and by that time their parents had gone to bed. They both retired straight to bed and so the subject of Wil wasn't broached again.

Chapter Three

Sunday breakfast was a bit of an institution at the Murrays' house, as presumably it was in most of the town's households. There was time to eat more leisurely than the other mornings and this Sunday was no exception. Jessie Murray had already set four places at the kitchen table and the bacon and sausages were keeping warm in the oven. Archie Murray was out in the back garden doing nothing in particular, perhaps just keeping out of the way until the breakfast was on the table. Jessie went to the bottom of the stairs and shouted up, 'Come on down, Stanley, you're breakfast's just about ready.'

'I'll be down in a minute,' was the response.

Fiona and her parents sat at the table and Stanley's breakfast was slipped into the oven until he emerged. The conversation was casual and Mum was asking about the dance.

Stanley appeared at the kitchen door. He had a towel wrapped round his waist. Round his neck he had several strings of beads, presumably from his mother's jewellery drawer. On his head was stuck an old lampshade. He started jumping up and down like an Indian warrior performing some traditional war dance and at the same time singing loudly, 'Down in the jungle, living in a tent, better than a prefab..., no rent.' His rendition was interspersed with 'oompaas' and animal noises as he cavorted around in a circle in the kitchen.

Fiona's stomach leapt up to near her throat in a moment of instant panic. She knew exactly what he was up to. Both Mum and Dad looked at Stanley as though he'd taken leave of his senses, though of course he was always good at acting the fool and tormenting Fiona.

'Come on and get your breakfast and stop this nonsense. What's up with you? What are you doing anyway?' Mum said, slightly irritated. 'You know I haven't time for this messing about on a Sunday when we're on our way to church.'

'Fee'll tell you what it's all about, won't you, Fee?'

Mum looked at Fiona whose appetite had suddenly gone. Her inside was throbbing with panic, but she managed to calmly say, 'Never mind him, he's only taking the mickey. It's nothing really. You know what he's like.'

'What's the war dance and the beads for?'

'I don't know. I don't know what he means,' lied Fiona. 'Do you want me to come to church with you?' she hastened on to ask, making a complete change of subject until she could think a bit more quickly. Stanley had caught her off guard. She hadn't intended to go to church at all, but she grasped at the first opportunity that presented itself to change the course of the conversation.

'Oh, yes, that would be nice. Yes, I'd like that, but you'd better get a move on. Have you a hat to wear?'

'I wasn't going to bother with one.'

'Please yourself, but I don't think it's right to go to church without a hat on. Why don't you wear that little black feather one of mine?'

'Alright then,' said Fiona, happy to fall in with her mum's wishes, simply to make any diversion from Stanley and his capers.

The church bells started ringing at quarter to eleven, calling the congregation. The only people out on the streets were those walking to church. The bells rang continuously while the three of them covered the distance between home and the church. They weren't long seated when the bells stopped ringing, signalling eleven o'clock and the start of the service.

Fiona enjoyed the hymns although she didn't pay too much notice to the minister's sermon. She was glad of the time to gather her thoughts together. She was annoyed with Stanley, but she realised that she would have to tell her parents about Wil and also her plans not to return home and work locally. Mum had already asked her when did she intend visiting her old junior school. It would be her mother's greatest wish to see Fiona teaching at the school down the road that she had attended as a child.

After lunch, Fiona decided she really ought to tell her parents, so while she was drying and putting away the dishes, she casually said to her mother, 'You know, Mum, I've got a boyfriend now back in Nottingham.'

'Oh, have you dear. Is he one of the students at college with you?'

'No, he's a doctor.'

'A doctor, well, well, well... Do you hear that Dad, our Fee's got a boyfriend and he's a doctor. What do you think of that then, Stanley? It's time you also got yourself a nice girlfriend. It would keep you from spending so much time and money at the bars.'

Stanley quickly replied, 'Yes, I know, Mum, but just wait until she tells you what his name is and where he comes from.' His eyes were shining with excitement and anticipation of what he knew would transpire next.

'So you know all about it already, do you? Leave her alone to tell us about him. What's his name then?'

'It's Wil. Actually it's Wilberforce Sankoli.'

'It's what?' Mum said incredulously.

'It's Wilberforce Sankoli and he comes from Africa, West Africa. Sierra Leone to be exact.'

The proverbial deathly hush fell. Mum's breath had been taken from her as though she'd had her head pushed under water. Then as she started to surface, mouth agape, she gasped, 'Are you telling me he's black? Is that what you're trying to say? Is this true?'

'Yes, Mum, he's black. Everybody who comes from West Africa is black. Didn't you know that?' Fiona sarcastically replied. She was bracing herself to be defensive.

'Don't you get smart with me, my lass, it's your mother you're talking to and don't forget that. I can tell you here and now, there's none of my family getting involved with anybody that's black. I've never heard the like of it. What's gotten into you? All these fancy ideas you young folk get nowadays when you go to college. It's just a passing phase. Wait and see, you'll soon find a nice local lad to go out with when you're home here for good and start to work.'

'You might as well realise that it's no passing fancy as you say. We love each other and I'm going to stay in Nottingham and teach there to be near Wil,' Fiona arrogantly replied.

'How old's this Wil?'

'He's thirty-two.'

'Fiona, can't you see he's far too old for you as well as everything else?'

Dad was quietly absorbing all this behind his *Sunday Post*. He obviously didn't intend getting drawn into the conversation. Stanley, his blue eyes wide and alert, was sitting in one of the armchairs by the fireside, opposite Dad and was clearly enjoying the drama surrounding him, presumably happy that he was only on the sidelines and not one of the participants.

'And what's the difference between Wil and anybody else, tell me?' Fiona asked, looking directly at her mother. They were both sitting on the couch in the lounge. Without waiting for a reply, she continued, 'It's because of the colour of his skin. That's it, isn't it? You're wrong you know, he's exactly the same as you and me.'

'Oh no, he's not the same, and you'd better believe that, my lass.'

'You'll change your mind when you meet him, Mum,' said Fiona, changing her tactic and opting for a more pleading approach.

'You get this straight here and now. You're not taking any black man here into my house. He's not coming here at all, ever. If you go against your Father's and my wishes and insist in going with him then we don't want anything to do with you either. No daughter of mine is going to carry on with a black man.'

Fiona noted that her mother was conveniently speaking for her father as well as herself. Poor Dad wasn't going to be allowed any opinion of his own.

'I'm not carrying on with him,' screamed Fiona. 'You're making it sound cheap and sordid. We're in love with each other. We're going to share a flat when I go back to Nottingham.'

'Don't tell my any more! That's enough! Share a flat indeed! And what's going to happen to you when he up tails and goes back home? No decent man would ever want you then. You've lost all sense of decency. Listen clearly to me, my lass because I don't want you to misunderstand and I'm not going to repeat myself, but you either forget all about this Wil chap or us. You can't have it both ways. And I'm warning you. Are you listening, Dad and Stanley, to what I'm saying? Not one word of this has to be breathed outside this house. Do you all hear? Is that clear? You're not bringing any shame to this doorstep. After all we've done for you. It's been the ruination of you away down there in England. I've said it now, and that's final.'

Fiona was by now very angry. 'Don't start on about all that again. I never asked you to do anything for me. You're narrow-minded and parochial. I thought you'd be above all the silly prejudices people have for coloured people. I expected you to be different and to understand. I thought you would want to see me happy.'

'Understand? What chance of happiness will you ever have? What do you know about him and his background? Nobody accepts a liaison of mixed races even, let alone mixed colours. Can't you see all this is a recipe for disaster and heartache? I've never been so affronted in all my life.'

Stanley, obviously enjoying himself, piped up, 'Do you think he was brought up in a mud hut? He might want to buy Fiona from us. Mind, I think they deal in cows, not hard cash. How many cows do you think you'd be worth, Fee?'

'Shut up, shut up both of you,' Fiona shouted angrily.

'You watch your tongue, Fiona. We won't have language like that in this house,' Mum added.

'Now, Jessie, I think that's enough said and this is the Sabbath as well,' Dad uncomfortably interrupted.

'All right, Archie. No more will be said about it. The subject's closed as far as I'm concerned and forgotten. It won't be mentioned again.'

Fiona raced upstairs to her bedroom, closed the door loudly and lay on the bed. She was furious, then tears of rage and frustration started to roll down her cheeks.

It had all gone horribly wrong. Nobody seemed to be on her side. Even her friends at college, including Judith, Margaret and Susan, voiced reservations about the relationship. Fiona couldn't understand why everybody took such a delight in pointing out all the pitfalls. Surely all relationships had pitfalls? If only she weren't so far away from Wil. She felt so unhappy and lonely. She needed his support and comfort more than ever before. Their love for each other was so strong it would ride the crest of all these problem waves. Surely the most important fact was their love for each other and being together. She decided she would show all the doubting Thomases the meaning of love and commitment. Why did everybody see everything so negatively? Perhaps it was a shock to her mother but once Wil and she had proved their love to be strong enough, she would surely come round and accept the situation.

Fiona was both hurt and angry. The anger fed her with a resilience which kept her spirits high. She felt her family were wrong and she would in time prove them wrong. Dad and Stanley would have nothing to say. Mum was the spokesperson in the Murray household. What Mum said went and both Dad and Stanley had always fallen in with this unspoken rule. They couldn't be called 'henpecked', it was just that they knew how not to rock the family boat… a case of almost anything for a quiet life. It was only Fiona who ever questioned Mum's authority.

Her tears had dried so she decided to take a walk along the beach to get out of the house. It was a warm Sunday afternoon. The streets were deserted, but the beach was full of activity.

She hurried down past the harbour where all the trawlers and seine-netters were lying idle, all waiting to go out to sea early next day. As she continued along Shore Street, leaving the harbour behind her, her pace slackened. Her impatience had set her off at a fast rate, faster than she could sustain. She passed down the row of neatly kept cottages built with large blocks of greyish- and brownish-coloured stone with their dormer windows protruding from the dark grey slate roofs. They were so much more attractive to her than the redbrick terraced ones of the Midlands. Maybe because they were the only kind of houses she'd been used to until she moved away. She left the houses behind and started to pick her way over the stony path on the dunes, carefully avoiding contact with the gorse and nettles which had colonised the once bare and sandy stretch. As she went over the dunes she slowed down even more. The loose sand made walking heavy going. Across the beach at the other side of the small bay, there on the headland, she could see the Covesea Skerries lighthouse, a tall imposing white column against the horizon of dark blue sky and dark green sea, beaming continuously its signal out to sea.

The sky was interspersed with white mountain-like cumulus cloud. The sandy beach was alive with Sunday picnickers happily enjoying the sea and sun. This peaceful picture was only interrupted by an occasional roar of throaty aeroplane engines taking off and landing over the bay. The bay lay in the flight path of planes from the nearby naval air base of HMS *Fulmar* and the RAF at Kinloss. The undesirable noise of the planes caused much debate in the town. On the positive side though, the bases provided work for quite a few locals and the town benefited from the spending power of the navy personnel and their families. Indeed many local girls had married young sailors and left the town for good.

Summer Sundays like this one always drew crowds of locals, especially from the inland towns and villages, to the beautiful sandy beach. The words 'beach, seaside, picnic' are magical to children. Summer wouldn't be the same without a day at the seaside. The foreshore was sprinkled with family groups relaxing in the warm sun. Fiona took off her shoes to walk barefoot along the sand and wove her way slowly along the beach dodging children of all ages. Some were actively building sandcastles with their newly acquired, brightly coloured buckets and spades. The tide was starting to flood in and fill castle moats with seawater. The occasional, more powerful wave would undermine some of the carefully built castles and wash them completely away. Others were paddling and splashing about in the cold, shallow water, jumping and playing in the waves. The water was decidedly cold, but the children running around in bathing suits didn't seem to notice. Their excitement insulated them from the cold water. All around were people looking happy and relaxed, eating sandwiches and either drinking tea from thermos flasks, or lemonade. The sound of excited children shouting to one another and laughter permeated the warm summer air. It seemed such a carefree day for all the picnic people on the beach.

Why is everybody else so happy? she thought as she wandered along the seashore. If only Wil were here to walk with me.

She considered walking all the way over to the base of the lighthouse, but laziness overtook her and she sat on the dry sand, put her arms round her knees and watched what was going on around, soaking up the mild, warm sun. She felt much calmer and thought about her mother's irrational behaviour. She made up her mind to cut her stay at home short and return to Nottingham. She had intended to stay at home until the middle of July, but that was three weeks away still. Now that her mother had taken a stand against her relationship with Wil, and openly disapproved, she realised that the atmosphere at home would not be a harmonious one. Dad and Stanley would be placed in the unenviable position of trying to remain neutral in Fiona's eyes, whereas in reality they would stick firmly behind Mum's decision.

Yes, Fiona thought to herself, to avoid any further confrontation and unpleasantness with Mum, I'll travel back to Nottingham and Wil on Wednesday night.

She could start to look for a permanent junior school position for September. Until then she could do temporary work. The money would come in handy. Also there was flat hunting with Wil to look forward to.

She rose and started back towards home. She picked her way through the happy crowd of people and headed inland over the steep, heavily overgrown gorse dune that separated the golf links from the beach. She put her shoes on again but had to pause several times to empty them of loose, dry sand before she descended on to the grass of the links. She crossed the narrow fairway in front of the clubhouse and reached the row of large houses on Stotfield Road. Many of these imposing dwellings had once been the summer residences of London gentry. They used to come to the town annually with their staff to enjoy the shooting season and play golf.

That evening, she told her parents of her decision to return to Nottingham. She also told them that although she loved them dearly and always would, she had made up her mind to follow her heart. It was on that unhappy note that she left home on the Wednesday, to return to Wil. Nevertheless, despite her chagrin, her spirits were high. She had so much to look forward to and so much planning to do. This was to be the exciting beginning of a new life and also the start of her career. She felt confident the breach with home was temporary. She'd eat away slowly at her mother, who would soon come to regret her hasty decision.

It was in that positive frame of mind that she stepped off the train on Thursday morning. Wil was there to meet her. She'd written to tell him of her earlier-than-expected return. How marvellous it was to see each other again after their first ever parting.

They lay in each other's arms at Wil's flat. They laughed; they joked; they made love; they drank coffee; they made love; they talked and talked; they made love; they ate toast and marmalade. The morning slipped past so fast. Nothing had changed between them. Both of them were intoxicated with happiness and desire for each other. Naturally Wil wanted to know why Fiona had come back so soon.

'Can I guess?' he asked. 'It's because your parents don't approve of me? That's it, isn't it?'

'You could say Mum wasn't very enthusiastic, but I don't see it as a major problem. She'll soon come round to the idea, you wait and see. And I missed you so much, I couldn't stay away any longer. Also, we've a lot of plans to set in motion.'

Fiona had the house to herself. The others had all gone home to their respective families and they were only due back to pack up sometime in August. She took a Saturday job in Woolworth's and during the week she waited on tables in a small café near the bus station in town, near the market and the Salvation Army. She had also telephoned the school at Netherfield and made an appointment to see the headmaster, who was unfortunately on holiday at the time and was not expected back for another couple of weeks.

Chapter Four

The week after her return Wil received a telegram from home which simply read: 'FATHER ILL STOP COME HOME SOONEST STOP REGINA'. A visibly upset Wil arrived at Fiona's that evening to say he would be leaving for home on the first available flight, consequently he would be travelling to London the next day. He had no other information as to what was wrong, but he felt sure that they would not have cabled him unless there was a serious problem. He had arranged with the hospital administration to be released on compassionate grounds immediately and he had also been able to book a flight on the plane in two days' time.

The following evening they parted for a second time at the railway station. Fiona felt totally dejected as the London-bound train pulled out of the station. Wil couldn't give her any indication of when he would return, but he hoped it would be within a month. There was only one flight a week to and from Sierra Leone.

She walked home slowly from the station that evening. She felt alone, lost and abandoned. She'd no one to turn to or confide in. If only one of the girls would return. She went to bed as soon as she got in and lay and cried and at last, exhausted, she fell asleep.

The following two weeks she worked all the extra hours she could at the café. It was hard work and she was not used to being on her feet all day. The Italian owner, Marco Caberelli, was a fat, ill-tempered and bad-mannered little man, but she was glad of the chance to tire herself out daily. There was less time for brooding when she was so physically exhausted. The work was not mentally taxing and she carried out her duties mechanically through that fortnight serving coffees, teas and snacks.

Both Judith and Margaret returned to the house during the second week. Judith had accepted a teaching post at a Nottingham school on Mansfield Road and was busy packing her things ready to move to a one-bedroom flat which she had rented as from September. Fiona was pleased to have Judith's company during this time. She knew that Judith didn't wholeheartedly approve of her relationship with Wil, but she also knew that Judith did like him. Her reservations were more concerned with how their relationship could develop in the longer term. She rather anticipated that once the initial strong sexual attraction subsided, they would drift apart naturally, but she was prudent enough not to express this to Fiona. She knew it would only hurt Fiona, who was at such a vulnerable emotional stage of the romance. Judith was Fiona's sole confidante so she knew about the plans for them to share a flat. Now that Wil had been called home, the plans for that had to be put on hold.

In the meantime Judith insisted that Fiona arrange to move in with her until Wil returned. After that they could look for a suitable place together. As it turned out, this proved unnecessary because Martin Russell, the student who was the new tenant of the house in The Park, agreed that Fiona could stay on until the end of September so long as she didn't object to sharing with him and another mechanical engineering student. Fiona was greatly relieved to know that while everything in her life was in limbo, at least she was assured of somewhere to stay.

When Wil had been gone over two weeks Fiona started to decline morally and physically. She was often working twelve hours a day at the café. However, she knew it was better for her to be working and earning some money rather than moping about the house all day. She was not used to long hours of physical work.

She had promised to help Judith one Sunday at her new flat. They wanted to clean out the kitchen cupboards and line them with paper. Judith had been steadily taking her belongings up to the flat by bus each time she went. The two of them had risen quite late that morning and it was nearly noon when they arrived at the flat off Mansfield Road, both laden with some of Judith's text books and college notes. They set about cleaning and tidying; Judith in the bedroom and Fiona in the kitchen. Later on in the afternoon they stopped to have something to eat.

'Fancy some cheese on toast and coffee?' Judith asked.

'That sounds great. Have you any tea though, I'd rather tea?'

'Yes, I have, but I've never known you to refuse coffee before. Are you feeling all right?'

'Yes, I'm fine, but you know the smell of coffee makes me feel a bit nauseous. I'd rather tea. I expect it's all that coffee I'm serving up at the café.'

'You sure you're all right? I have thought you've seemed a bit off colour lately.'

'I just feel a bit weak and dizzy sometimes. I expect it's working all them hours lately that's doing it.'

'Sounds more like you're pregnant to me than overwork,' Judith blurted out.

'Pregnant? No, I hadn't thought of that one,' Fiona half laughingly replied.

'Well, when was your last period? Go on, tell me.'

'I can't really remember.'

'Try and remember then, Miss Murray, it could be important.'

Immediately Fiona's expression started to change and she started to think.

'Come on, Fiona. You're not late, are you?' Judith could feel a sudden panic come over her as she started to grasp the seriousness of the conversation and its implications. 'Is there any possibility that you could be pregnant? Have you and Wil been... Well, have you?'

'Yes, we have. Oh, God, let me think back now. What's the date today?'

'Twenty-first of August.'

'I haven't had a period for ages now, but I've not really thought anything about it what with the emotional stress of the exams and then the row at home.'

'Can you think of the date though?'

Fiona sat with her chin cupped in her fists and was thinking. 'When did we sit our first exam? Was it the fourth of June?'

'Yes, it was.'

'I remember now, I had a period then. Let me see, I came on just before that exam. It must have been the end of May.'

'But that's months ago! Nothing since then?'

'No.'

'You certain?'

'Yes, I'm sure.'

'Fiona, you could be nearly three months pregnant, do you know that?'

'Oh Judith, I'd never thought of that.' Fiona was visibly shaken. She even looked surprised.

'What are you going to do then? What if Wil doesn't come back?'

'Of course he'll be back. Don't say a thing like that.'

'What are you going to do then? How do you think he'll react?'

'I don't know, I really don't know.'

'Maybe before we jump to any conclusions though, you ought to find out for certain. With a bit of luck it might be all the stress and overwork that's upset your cycle. Have you had any cravings, or any other possible symptoms of pregnancy?'

'Just going off coffee and feeling slightly nauseous.'

'I think you'd better go and have a chat to the medical officer at college to find out for sure. I think the sooner the better. Do you want me to come with you? You know I'm free any time if you do.'

'Yes, I could do with some moral support. You don't mind coming with me? I'll make an appointment as soon as I can.'

'You can count on me, Fiona. Why don't we go tomorrow on the off-chance he'll see you?'

'No, better make it Tuesday and I can let grumpy old Marco know I'm having time off. You know what he'd be like if I didn't pitch tomorrow morning, or if I want time off without giving him warning.'

On Tuesday morning the doctor confirmed that Fiona was about twelve weeks' pregnant.

Since Sunday, Fiona had had time to contemplate her situation. Wil wasn't there to share her problem and she consequently only had Judith for support. Although she felt sure that Wil would stand by her, it did mean that everything had changed. She'd no longer be able to take on a teaching post now that she was pregnant. If only Wil would return. She was certain he would – but always a nagging little voice in the back of her mind repeated Judith's words, 'What if Wil doesn't come back? ' What would she do if he didn't return, or wasn't supportive? How could she manage now without a job and having a child to support? A coloured child at that. Her mother would certainly disown her now. In fact she'd not even be able to tell her mother.

That week she carried on working not knowing what was going to happen to her. She could stay on at the café for as long as she could. At least she had that she could depend on. Although these negative thoughts did come to Fiona, she still felt sure that once Wil returned, they would work things out together. After all, they were deeply in love with each other.

At last, on Saturday, the twenty-seventh of August, at precisely midday, Wil appeared at Woolworth's. He'd travelled back from Sierra Leone and got into Nottingham only that morning. Fiona was ecstatic! She could hardly believe it was really him. She hurriedly arranged to change her lunch hour with one of the other casual Saturday assistants so that she could leave immediately with him. She should have been on lunch break only at one o'clock. She preferred the one o'clock lunch hour, but she simply couldn't wait another hour to find out all Wil's news.

In the hour they had together they walked up to the Castle grounds. Sadly, Wil's father had suffered a heart attack. Three days after Wil's arrival home he suffered a second, fatal attack. Wil had indeed been fortunate enough to have arrived home in time to see his father alive. Wil looked strained, sad and tired. Part of it was the long journey, but he was mainly drained by the grief he was suffering over his father's death. There had also been the trauma of the funeral. He hadn't yet had time to let the reality of all these events sink in.

'Darling, my darling Fiona!' Wil was evidently overjoyed to see her again. 'It's wonderful to be back with you again; but you look so thin and tired. What have you been up to since I've been gone? You look as though you've been working far too hard. I've been and spoken to old Johnstone in administration this morning and I'm back on duty Monday morning. I'll go and get something for a special celebration dinner at my place tonight. Stay overnight and we'll have all day tomorrow together as well, before I start work and we can catch up on some lost time.'

Already Fiona was feeling on top of the world again. They kissed and embraced excitedly and then it was time for her to return to work for the afternoon.

'Until tonight, my darling. Come round straight from work and I'll be waiting for you.'

'No, I must go and tell Judith I won't be home tonight, or at least leave a note for her if she's not in, so she'll know where I am. I'll be straight round after that. Then we can celebrate together. I've also got some news for you, darling,'

'Can it wait until tonight?'

'Yes, of course it can,' she happily replied.

Fiona returned to work different, happy and confident. What a mental transformation in that hour. Half of her nagging doubts had gone. Wil had returned. She even started to think enthusiastically about her pregnancy. She was sure Wil would understand and that they would be able to work things out together. The problem didn't seem quite so insurmountable after all. Wil still belonged to her, she was sure of that.

Chapter Five

Wil was eagerly awaiting her arrival that night. He'd prepared supper and had a bottle of red wine waiting to be uncorked. They embraced and clung to each other and confirmed their everlasting love for each other, both admitting the misery of their separation.

'Here's to us!' Wil proposed as he poured wine into two empty glasses.

'Yes, to us,' Fiona toasted and held her glass up to touch his. 'I suppose it's in order for pregnant women to take alcohol?' she added mischievously.

'Yes, in moderation, there's not really any harm. Why do you… you're not saying… you're not… are you? Are you? You saying you're pregnant?' he eventually gasped. His big brown eyes looked at her in astonishment.

She simply nodded.

He put down his glass and took her gently in his arms. He was looking so proud and whispered, 'This is marvellous news. My little Fiona's going to have a baby! This is just wonderful after the heartache of losing my father. Fiona, it'll be a boy, I'm sure. He's coming into the world to take the place left by my father. You've heard of the birth that follows after a death, haven't you? Are you sure? When's the baby due? Are you feeling all right? You'll have to look after yourself now. Quick, let's add a new toast to the baby,' as he excitedly lifted his glass up again.

'Yes, I'm sure. The doctor at the campus examined me last Tuesday and said I was about twelve weeks. That means the baby should be due early in February.'

Fiona was now overjoyed. Wil was obviously delighted. 'You're pleased then? Not cross or angry?'

'Angry? What's there to be angry about? Life's really good to me, first meeting you and now so soon a baby on the way. What else could a man want, tell me? My happiness is almost complete.'

'Almost? Why almost? Is there a problem?'

'Losing my father has created quite a few problems, my darling. I've had to make some plans when I was at home and I was saving them up to tell you about them all tonight and tomorrow. Now you've presented me with a new scenario which has to be taken into consideration.'

'What do you mean?'

'Come, my darling, let's eat supper first before it dries up and drink our wine and then we can settle down and I'll tell you all that's happened to me.'

Wil's only sister, Regina, had cabled him when his father took the heart attack. Luckily, Wil had arrived home before the second, fatal attack. It had been a great consolation to him, to be able to be with his father for the few days preceding his death. His father had been lucid but bedridden at the family home. The old man had acknowledged his impending demise and had frankly discussed family-related matters with Wil. Wil was the only son and was duty-bound to carry out his father's dying wishes.

Wil was to return home and take over as head of the family and keep his father's medical practice going. He had always known that this would be his future role. He just hadn't anticipated his father's death coming about so soon. He was enjoying his life in medicine in England and at the same time was always gaining additional medical skills which he would eventually use when the time came for him to return home. He had always hoped that he would work with his father in the practice and slowly take over, allowing his father a period of semi-retirement from his work. Now his sudden untimely death had presented Wil with a *fait accompli* which necessitated immediate action.

'You mean you'll be leaving here for good and going home?' she whispered, clearly stunned by the dramatic turn of events.

'Yes, darling. My carefree days of life in the civilised First World have ended. I've got to face the real work of Third World poverty and all its medical problems. I've promised my father and also I'm the only son and it's my duty to look after my mother and provide for her and keep up the family home and medical practice.'

'What about us and the baby, Wil? When do you have to leave?' Fiona was starting to be overcome by a feeling of desperation. She'd never ever considered the possibility that he'd be leaving England and going back to work in Africa. This was totally unexpected. Never in all her twenty-two years had Fiona's emotions had to spread the complete gamut that they had done over the past few short months. She'd gone through feelings of ecstasy, despair, happiness, devastation, sadness, loss, love, hate… they'd all been part of her involvement with Wil.

'I promised my father before he died that I'd return home immediately. I've only returned to the General to work my notice and tidy up my affairs. When we discussed it all of course I was expecting him to be alive for a much longer time. I was expecting us to be able to work together, or at least I would have worked under his supervision if he wasn't able to play an active part in the practice any more. I was expecting to benefit from his leadership and advice. All that changed when he died, but I still need to return home immediately and I'll now have to find my own feet. It would have made it so much easier for me if he'd been there with me for even a few months.

'I spoke to the administration at the hospital today and I've already tendered my resignation which is effective in September. They were very understanding though and said I could be released in two weeks' time under the circumstances and also because I have quite a lot of accumulated holidays owing to me.

'I thought I could go in two or three weeks' time. That should give me enough time to organise everything here. Now, my darling, you're presenting me with your news and that's going to change things somewhat.

'I had planned to ask you to marry me and if you agreed then we could get engaged before I went home. I wanted to give you the chance to consider whether or not you wanted to come to Sierra Leone and live there with me. I thought that you could have worked here for a year and during that time I would concentrate on establishing myself at home and taking over the practice. Now, what do you think we should do? What do you want to do, my darling?'

'Do you still want to marry me, Wil? Please be honest with me. You're not just saying this because of the baby, are you?'

He drew her very close to him and tilted her chin up towards his face with his finger. 'Come now, Fiona darling. You're being oversensitive. Of course I want to marry you. I love you, don't you understand that? I want you to be my wife. I just wanted you to have time to think about it carefully before making a decision. You know it's not everybody who would want to give up the city life and go and live in the jungles of Africa. I know what I'm returning to. It's a completely unknown quantity for you, Fiona.'

'All I know, is I want to be with you wherever you are, my darling. I don't need time to think. I'm only happy now when I'm with you. Go on then, ask me!'

'Ask you what?'

'To marry you, silly!' She was now laughing and fast regaining her sense of humour. 'I want to be proposed to in real romantic fashion!'

'You mean I've to ask your father how many cows he wants for you? That's African fashion.'

'Don't be ridiculous. Don't you know you're supposed to kneel at my feet and ask? That's how it's done in all the romantic novels I've read. If you do that, then I'll accept. You see, I come pretty cheap. You get me free of charge, so to speak. Just think how many cows you'll save!'

'Now, let's see,' he cleared his throat and coughed. He put on a bit of an act and asked, 'Please, Fiona, will you marry me?' and hastily added, 'can't we dispense with the kneeling down bit, I don't want to dirty the knees of my trousers and I'd like an answer in the next ten seconds as well. This is a once in a lifetime offer you know!'

'I'll have to give this careful consideration,' she joked.

He then started counting, 'One, two, three, four, five, six, seven, eight.'

She jumped up in the air and put her arms round his neck, looked lovingly into his eyes and whispered, 'I'll be honoured to be your wife.'

They embraced and kissed. This was surely one of the happiest moments in her life. Last weekend she had had such nagging doubts; she had been tired, she'd found out she was pregnant, then today everything changed. He was happy about the baby and he wanted to marry her. She was almost afraid to fall asleep that night, lest the magic of the evening should slip away.

The next day they discussed some plans for their future. Wil wanted to return home as soon as he could. They decided to get married in the Registry Office and after that he would fly out to Sierra Leone. In the meantime Fiona would remain in Nottingham, get all the necessary travel documents and injections. She would have to follow on afterwards on her own, perhaps a month later. Wil said that in the month without her he could concentrate on his work and also break the news to his family that he had married a foreigner.

'I've never thought of myself as a foreigner,' mused Fiona. 'Do you think your folk will be happy about us? Did you tell them about me when you were at home?'

'No, I didn't. I couldn't be sure that you would come home with me and even if you did agree, I was working along the assumption that it might be a while. I hadn't anticipated the baby coming along so soon. I think my mother might take a little time to come to accept the situation. She'll naturally be disappointed I'm not marrying one of the local girls. I don't foresee too many problems though. What are you going to do about your family now?'

'I don't know. How do you think I should handle it?'

'That's a tricky one for me to advise on. I don't know your parents and you'll have to do what you think is best under the circumstances. Why don't you discuss it with Judith?'

'Yes, I think I'll do that. I was going to ask her to come along to the ceremony as a witness anyway. Will you get your friend, Ismail, to come as well? We'll need both of them as witnesses. We'd better go along to the Registry Office soon because I think there are certain formalities to be gone through. I think there's a notice period and also we've to make a booking.'

Three weeks later they married at the Nottingham Registry Office. Judith and Ismail came with them. Afterwards the wedding group of only four proceeded to a lunchtime celebration. Three days later the newly-weds had to part. Fiona was left to attend to all the necessary outstanding documentation required for her departure. There was the smallpox, yellow fever and typhoid injections and certificates to be obtained and a passport in her new married name of Sankoli.

For the short time prior to her departure to Sierra Leone, Fiona moved in with Judith, who had started her teaching job. Fiona would also have been starting out on her teaching career had it not been for the series of dramatic events which had now changed her life. She deliberated on what she ought to tell her parents, or whether or not she ought to tell them anything. Judith felt, and Fiona agreed, that her parents deserved at least to know that she was leaving the country and where they could contact her if necessary.

'Your mother may not want to accept Wil into the family,' argued Judith, 'but I do think it's your duty to let her know your address.'

After several abortive attempts, she eventually composed a letter to her parents telling them that she had married Wil and was leaving within a couple of weeks to join him in Sierra Leone. She decided not to mention her pregnancy. She would take one step at a time. She gave them her new address. She sent her love, hoped they would forgive her for going against their wishes and hoped to hear from them.

Mum did not reply to Fiona's letter.

Unbeknown to Fiona, her mother was devastated by the news. She had had no idea whatsoever that this could be the turn of events following Fiona's tantrum and hasty departure back in June. Guilt ate into her. Had it been a direct result of her opposition that Fiona had deliberately taken this drastic step? Was she deliberately trying to punish her? Had she perhaps done this just to prove a point? Whatever happened, no one must know that Fiona had married an African. What a disgrace and humiliation if relations, friends and neighbours were to find out. The family would be the laughing stock of the town. The day the letter came, Archie and Stanley were given it to read for themselves and then were instructed by Jessie that no word of this had to be breathed outside the house. They were sworn to secrecy. This scandal had to be contained within their own four walls. When people enquired after Fiona, they would say that she had taken a post with a voluntary educational organisation which provided young, newly qualified teachers with the opportunity to work in underdeveloped countries and that she had been assigned to Sierra Leone.

Secretly, Jessie was bitter and heartbroken and from that day on Fiona's name was seldom mentioned in the Murray household.

Chapter Six

In the evenings before her departure Fiona would sometimes sit with Judith and chat about what life in Africa might be like. Wil had never really discussed his home and family much with her. She knew that there was his mother and that he had an older married sister, Regina, with a family of three and she lived in Freetown and her husband was some kind of government officer. Apart from those very basic facts, Sierra Leone was a completely unknown quantity.

'What if you've to live in a mud hut, Fiona?' laughed Judith.

Fiona also laughed at the idea. 'I think they're a bit more civilised than that now.'

'You know it's called "the white man's grave"?'

'No, I didn't. I wonder why?'

'It was named that by the British press because nearly all the white folk who went out there died from the conditions and the climate there.'

'Charming! How do you know that anyway?'

'I asked Robert Bradwell at work today if he knew anything about Sierra Leone. He's our geography teacher. He didn't know all that much about the place, but he looked up a book and found out it's in the tropical rain forest belt. You know, real jungle country and the natives there still practise cannibalism. Better watch yourself out in the dark at night lest you end up in a stew-pot!'

'You're as bad as my brother Stanley. That's the sort of thing he'd tell me. It won't be like that at all. Anyway, I'll write to you soon and tell you if it's true or not.'

'You will write me, won't you and let me know how you get on?'

'Of course I will.'

'And let me know as soon as you've had the baby?'

Fiona took Judith's teasing very half-heartedly. She wasn't expecting her life to be dramatically different. It would probably be warmer, being nearer the equator, that much she knew and that the inhabitants would be black.

On Tuesday, the eighteenth of October, Fiona set off on the first leg of the start to her new life. She'd never been abroad before, let alone flown anywhere. She was nervous and excited as the plane took off from London. By the time touchdown at Lisbon came she found she was quite enjoying the flight. The next stop was Las Palmas where she would be in transit overnight.

Mid-afternoon the plane landed at Gando airport on the island of Gran Canaria, one of the seven islands belonging to the Spanish archipelago. These islands sprawled across nearly 400 miles of the North Atlantic off the North African coast. A bumpy bus ride took passengers and crew north to the island's capital, Las Palmas, the largest city in the Canaries.

Fiona viewed the strange surroundings from her window seat as the bus bounced over the uneven road which in places appeared to be squeezed precariously close to the seashore by an inland mountain formation. They passed banana plantations along the route and the local inhabitants reminded her of peasants. The men and boys were poorly dressed in cotton shirts and trousers and wore wide-brimmed straw hats to protect them from the searing heat of the hot sun. The women all appeared old and were dressed in long black clothes. Many had their long black, or grey, hair covered with black lace squares as though they'd just attended mass. Some of the women sat outside their humble Spanish-style houses crocheting fine cotton lace.

Once at the hotel, she seized the opportunity to wander along the main shopping area before darkness fell. The shopkeepers all spoke enough English to enable her to make a few purchases. She bought a beautiful postcard to send to Judith. It pictured a Spanish dancer and was made from brightly coloured material and embroidery. She'd no Spanish money, but that was not a problem. The shops eagerly accepted British pounds. The Indian shopkeepers tempted her with cheap cameras and watches which bore neither purchase tax nor import duties. Liquor was also cheap. She sat at one of the outside cafés and watched with interest the passers-by as she drank a cool orange squash. She soon realised the inhabitants of Las Palmas were leading a different lifestyle to the rural population. The peasants she passed on the way from the airport were working the land and were very poor, probably eking out a meagre existence from agriculture. Las Palmas had the benefit of a vibrant tourist industry to enable its inhabitants to attain a higher standard of urban life, more in keeping with holiday resorts. It was easy to distinguish the pale-skinned European visitors from the local bronzed beach beauties. Only a few hours on the island, yet she left next morning with vivid, yet vague impressions of the Canaries.

The first stop next day was the Gambia. Her first step on African soil, she thought, as the plane began its descent. The stewardess warned of the metal runway there and not to be alarmed by the noise created by the aeroplane's wheels taxiing on the runway after touchdown. The noise probably wouldn't have alarmed Fiona, who wasn't a seasoned air traveller. The plane got nearer and nearer the ground. She could see the palm treetops and even identify huts and people. Then they touched down on African soil to refuel.

The rush of hot humid air took her by surprise as she stepped out onto the steps and then the ground. The passengers made their way to the small airport building. Several vendors with local crafts had their goods displayed outside on rush mats. Fiona looked eagerly around her.

So this is Africa! she thought.

The vendors were trying to sell their crafts and carvings but she didn't understand them, and merely smiled. The intense heat had taken her by surprise. It seemed somehow heavy and oppressive. It was certainly much hotter than she had expected. She hoped she would enjoy this state of permanently being warm.

Next stop... Sierra Leone! When the plane landed at Lungi Airport, there was Wil to meet her and help her through customs. Oh, how marvellous it was to see him again. It was such a relief that he had met her at the airport to help with getting through the formalities of immigration. She certainly felt foreign to all that was going around her. Although English was being spoken, she couldn't understand what was being said. Everybody spoke too fast and the words and accent confused her.

'You'll soon learn to understand and speak the Creole language. It's just Pidgin English!' Wil assured her.

A waiting bus, which had seen better days, took them away from Lungi airport to catch the ferry to Freetown. Wil explained that the airport lay on the opposite side of a wide natural bay from the capital city of Freetown necessitating a ferry journey across the Rokel estuary.

The bus ride was uncomfortable. The vehicle felt as though it had no suspension. All along the sides of the road were native huts and shacks and small black children waved a welcome to the bus passengers as they passed. They looked so happy... smiling with broad grins and white, white teeth.

On the ferry, Wil and Fiona felt more private. He was anxious to know how she was. How wonderful it was to be together. She was torn between hanging on to Wil or looking all around her to absorb as much as she could of her new surroundings and her new country of residence.

During the ferry crossing, which took approximately forty minutes, she could see Freetown in the distance. Lush green hills rose out from the sea dotted with buildings visible through the dense vegetation. Wil explained to her that Sierra Leone took its name from these mountains surrounding the harbour at Freetown, the literal translation being 'Lion Mountains'. It was a semi-overcast day but very hot and humid. Smells wafted over the sea and permeated the air as they neared the quay. She couldn't identify them. They were not offensive, but certainly different to anything she knew. Later on, she was to find out that it was a mixture of palm oil and the aroma of the flowers with even a hint of garbage and rotting vegetation.

Wil told her in the taxi which took them through the bustling Freetown streets that they would stay overnight and fly up country the following day. The taxi dropped them at the City Hotel in the centre of town. The hotel had been built in the 1920s and was showing outward signs of dilapidation. The bar was very popular and appeared to be full of local worthies.

The hotel's beauty lay in its colonial-style architectural design. It was now a relic of a bygone era. Inadequately small compared to new hotels, it looked more like a large English country mansion. Attention had been paid to its proportion and symmetry; its front was recessed behind a columned verandah which extended up to the first floor; three rectangular dormer windows completed the front elevation. Sadly, with age, it had declined and was suffering the growing reputation of being a seedy meeting place for those with little better to do than sit around drinking all day.

The open drainage system surprised her. Fiona was used to gutters at the sides of the roads, here, there were deep open ditches which were quite hazardous to pedestrians. She later learned that these deep open sewers were needed to cope with the volume of run-off after tropical storms. Rapid downpours were common in the rainy season; then these open drains quickly became raging torrents of water as the vast quantities of water gushing off the roads channelled into them.

The hotel room was very basic but it had air-conditioning, something Fiona had never come across before. Wil had booked in earlier and left the machine running so for the first time that day she felt the benefit of some cool air. A combination of the humidity, the travelling and the excitement of the journey and their reunion left Fiona feeling slightly weak and jaded. At last, though, they were alone together. In no time at all the cool air of the bedroom and an iced drink revived her. They lay on the bed, held each other close, kissed, cuddled, laughed, joked and best of all, made passionate love. Afterwards they lay and talked, exchanging news and discussing the events since their parting nearly a month ago.

Wil was enthusiastic about his work and said he was settling in. He had worked out a weekly schedule with the help of his father's assistant, Kissie. She was a nurse and was also his receptionist at the Kenema surgery. She'd worked with his father for ten years and was proving to be invaluable. Of course, he had known Kissie for many years, too. Work at the surgery and at the Kenema Hospital, where he also worked two days a week, was very different to conditions he was used to at the General in Nottingham. She could detect his enthusiasm for his new work. He seemed relaxed and happy to be back home again and working with his own people. Although he'd been to school and medical school in Britain, he'd always returned during holidays so he had maintained a group of friends and contact with extended family members. Apart from being busy at the surgery, he said visitors, all happy to see him and to wish him well, had constantly inundated the house. Everybody was pleased that he would be taking over his father's work. His father's death had denied the locals of a well-loved and highly respected physician. Unfortunately, professional blacks, such as doctors, lawyers and accountants, hardly ever returned to the remote African interiors, preferring instead the more sophisticated capital cities when and if they ever returned from abroad. Most of them preferred to practise in Europe or the States. This was the unfortunate state of affairs in most West African countries, and the large rural populations had little access to the expertise of skilled medical attention.

'Did you get in touch with home?'

'Yes, I wrote them and told them we had got married and gave them the Kenema box number as my address. I didn't mention anything about being pregnant though. I thought Mum might have written me before I came away, but nothing. I expect she's just taking a bit of time to get used to the idea. I'm sure she'll come round soon. I don't see it as a major problem. How did your mother react when you told her you were married?'

'She was quite surprised. Naturally a bit put out that it was all done behind her back and that she didn't have the benefit of a big wedding celebration. She's looking forward to meeting you though. She would have preferred that I'd married one of the local girls, but she's admitted that as long as it's what I want, then she's happy for us both. There's great preparations going on at home for your arrival. Mother will be there at the airport waiting for us to arrive tomorrow. I expect the house will be full of visitors for weeks to come wanting to meet you. Regina's also very excited about meeting you.'

'That's your sister, isn't it?'

'Yes. She's picking us up tonight to go out with them. She'll be round at about seven with Brima. You'll meet them both then.'

'Is that her husband? What did you say his name was?'

'It's Brima. Tell me now, how's this big boy coming on in here?' as he gently rubbed her stomach. 'You keeping well? No more sickness?'

'No, we're both fine. Fighting fit I'd say. You know I'm five months already. I hope you won't be disappointed if it's a girl. Can you see I'm spreading out all around?'

Her waistline had disappeared, but otherwise her pregnancy wasn't particularly noticeable. She had arrived wearing a shift-style summer dress, which conveniently disguised her expanded waistline.

'Do they know I'm pregnant?'

'Yes, the family know and are very happy. It's a good sign to them of fertility. Africans are still in favour of large families. It'll take a long time for my people to come to accept the benefits of the small families that they have in the western world. The concept of large families, the family unit and caring for the extended family group are still of paramount importance here. You're going to have to get used to living with all the family out here. I hope you won't mind that'.

'No, I don't think I'll mind at all. I'll probably be glad of the company when you're out at work all day. Do you think I'll be able to understand them? I couldn't catch a word of what you were saying to the customs official.'

Wil laughed. 'Of course you'll understand them. It won't take long. Wait and see.'

Chapter Seven

It was nearly half past seven when Brima and Regina turned up. Fiona would soon learn that time in Africa wasn't a particularly important aspect of its culture. In fact she was to learn later on that the local languages had no translation for the word 'time'. Only the western world was obsessed with time and timekeeping. Urgency and stress were not problems for the average Sierra Leonean. Their concerns were more to do with poverty, disease and surviving from day to day.

The evening turned out to be extremely enjoyable. Brima and Regina were a delightful couple and gave Fiona the impression that they were very proud to have a European sister-in-law. Regina, in keeping with her name, was lavishly dressed in an almost regal blue and gold-coloured cotton native outfit, complete with matching headdress. She was plump but the full-length skirt and the height of the headdress gave her an air of elegance. She had a round, friendly face and a happy disposition. She wanted to know so much about life in Britain while Fiona wanted to know about life in Sierra Leone.

Regina apologised to Fiona for being unable to accommodate them at their house. It was presently full with some of Brima's relations. The two girls had pleaded to come and meet Fiona, but it was too late in the evening and they had to be up for school early in the morning.

'You have three children, haven't you?' enquired Fiona.

'Yes, I have my own two, Priscilla and Lahai, but in addition I have Poppy during school terms. She's Kissie's daughter, you know, father's assistant. She's seven and comes to school here in Freetown. The schools are better here. She goes home for the holidays though. You'll see her at Christmas. She's good company for Priscilla as there's only a year between them. Priscilla's six now and Lahai, my baby boy, is only three.'

Dinner had just been served when a huge electric storm broke. The booming, rolling peals of thunder drowned conversation and the accompanying flashes of lightning lit up the black, star-studded sky. Then the lights went out. Fiona was secretly terrified. Never had she encountered such a violent thunderstorm. Candles were quickly lit at all the tables in the club.

'Do you often get these storms?' she asked Regina.

'Oh yes, they're regular occurrences, but only in the rainy season. The rains are nearly at an end now and we're just coming into the dry season. You'll get used to them, but it's a nuisance when the electricity goes as well.'

The storm made the club an eerie room. There they all were, eating in romantic candlelight with the heavy rain clattering down onto the corrugated iron roof. The not-so-distant thunder rolling restlessly all around, and the vivid lightning flashes streaking across of the sky directly to the ground, lighting up inside and out momentarily, then plunging them back to the dimness of the flickering candles. Fiona shivered, but not because it was cold. Indeed, the rain had reduced the heat to a more comfortable temperature. The storm had been preceded by gusts of wind which had set the open windows and doors banging about on their hinges and the curtains flapping uncontrollably about. The waiters had quickly closed the doors and tucked the curtains into the grills on the windows before the onset of the driving rain could be blown inside.

The storm blew itself out within twenty minutes and the rain continued to fall, though much more steadily and softly. The electricity didn't come on again and they ended their evening by candlelight.

The drive back to the City Hotel was unusual because of the lack of electricity. Most of the dwellings and shops they passed were twinkling like stars with candles or oil lamps.

'I wish you were staying longer,' Regina sadly admitted when they stopped to let them out. 'It would be so much fun to have you here for a few weeks to show you around and introduce you to my friends and Brima's relatives. You'd love to see our beach as well. I know that all the Europeans here love to go and swim and sunbathe on the beach. We couldn't see it from the club tonight, but our Lumley beach is very beautiful. Promise me, dear brother, that you'll bring her back on holiday soon?'

Fiona felt happy that she had made a friend of Regina. They retired to bed immediately and lay in the candlelight. They would be together now for ever, they promised each other that. Their lovemaking was urgent; as if they wanted to make up the lost time they had suffered. Eventually they lay back sweating and exhausted. The air conditioning wasn't working due to the power failure, consequently the air was hot in the room and Fiona began to feel breathless. She wanted to open the window to let the air circulate.

'You can't do that here, my darling. Not here.'

'Why not?'

'We'd be eaten alive by the mosquitoes and that would be a lot worse than putting up with the heat. We can only open the windows when we've got mosquito nets and there aren't any here.'

'What's a mosquito net like then?' said Fiona, suddenly realising that there was an awful lot about living in Sierra Leone that was unfamiliar.

'You know the four-poster beds they used to have in England in the old days? The ones with curtains all round them? Well, mosquito nets are a bit like that. It's a bit like sleeping with a tent round the bed, but the tent is made of white netting. That stops the mozzies getting into bed with you. You'll be pleased to know we've got one over our bed at home. You'll see tomorrow what they're like.'

Fortunately, at about half past one the lights and air conditioning were suddenly activated with the re-instatement of the electricity supply. That soon cooled the room temperature down and she fell fast asleep, wrapped in her husband's loving arms.

Next day they boarded a very small aeroplane to take them on their journey up country. Fiona's confidence ebbed somewhat at the sight of the small plane and even more so when the turbaned Indian pilot took to starting the engine by going out and frantically turning the propeller on the nose of the plane manually prior to take-off. The small plane shook and rattled. Fiona soon began to enjoy the flight however, more so even than she had the much larger plane on the international flight. They flew at a much lower altitude enabling her to have a bird's-eye view of the countryside below. The treetops didn't seem to be so far beneath her and the natives and their huts were clearly visible. They touched down at Bo and then again at Kenema, their destination.

When they got off the plane there was the welcoming party awaiting their arrival. Mama Nkozi was first in line. Then came Kissie, followed by an entourage of relations and friends, servants and children. All had names Fiona couldn't hope to pronounce, let alone remember! They just couldn't seem to contain their excitement at meeting her. Fiona immediately felt like a visiting dignitary. Everybody had turned out in their 'Sunday best' to welcome and meet her. Their eager, friendly welcome was indeed reassuring. Mother-in-law, or Mama Nkozi, as Wil had already told her she was known as, embraced her enthusiastically.

'Welcome to Kenema and to our family. We hope you will be very happy here with my dear son, Wilberforce. Come, let's get your luggage and go home. I expect you will be tired after your long journey.'

It took fully half an hour before the welcoming party settled down and everybody started to drift off to their cars. Mama Nkozi was clearly in charge. A large dominating woman whose authority was unquestioned, Fiona noted. This was a woman used to giving orders and being in command. She was stout, perhaps even fat, with a huge protruding bottom and matronly chest. She, like all the other women present, wore a beautiful, full-length, native costume complete with elaborate matching headdress. The Sierra Leonean ladies certainly were imposing and elegant in their national dress. Fiona realised that by comparison her simple shift-style cotton, knee-length dress made her look very ordinary. She wondered if they always looked as if they were going to attend a ball.

They all made their way to a large Mercedes Benz. The driver, introduced as Lansana, leapt out of the driving seat and quickly opened all the doors and loaded the luggage into the boot. He also greeted Fiona with enthusiasm. A short drive took them home. Fiona's first impression was one of relief. She had secretly worried about the possibility that they might actually live in a mud hut! She hadn't had the courage to ask such a question outright, lest it caused Wil embarrassment, or made her feel ridiculous. When the car came to a halt outside the veranda of the tin-roofed bungalow it was immediately surrounded by a group of natives, all eager to meet the new 'madam', as Fiona found out she was being referred to.

There were only the four of them for dinner that night – Mama Nkozi, Kissie, Will and Fiona. Kissie was obviously treated as one of the family and lived with them. The four of them were waited upon by a barefooted youth, Saffa, who was dressed in khaki shorts and matching tunic. He was referred to as 'the small boy'. Mama Nkozi explained to Fiona that Saffa was under the supervision of the cook, Aruna, similar to an apprenticeship. One day he would hope to get a cook's position. In the meantime, however, he performed the more menial culinary tasks and waited on the table. He was courteous and when spoken to always addressed Mama Nkozi as 'madam'.

'All the staff will call you "madam" also,' Wil told Fiona later that night. 'They won't ever refer to you by your name. That would not be proper in our society. Servants are servants and must be treated accordingly. They must show their employers proper respect.'

This attitude somewhat surprised Fiona, but then her family had never been sufficiently affluent to employ servants. Only the nobility in Britain had servants, or the very rich.

'You'll be left on your own here for a bit tomorrow,' Wil said when they were being served coffee. 'Kissie and I will be at the surgery and Mama will be at the shop. We'll all be back for lunch between noon and two o'clock though, so that will break the day for you.'

'That's fine by me. Is there anything I can do when you're all out?'

Mama Nkozi said, 'No, no, my dear. I'll leave the orders for the boys in the morning. You just settle yourself in and have a relaxing day. Throw your dirty washing into the bath in the morning and Kelly will see to it. Wil, you must help your wife with the house routine.'

'Anything you need,' Kissie interrupted, 'when we're out, just ask. Kelly will be busy around the house in the morning doing the work and both Aruna and Saffa will be around, probably out in the kitchen preparing lunch. We have breakfast together at eight, but if you want to sleep in, you don't have to get up then.'

'I think I'll get up with you all, as long as I'm not in the way. At least I can see you all off. What time do you leave?'

'Around quarter to nine is our usual time. Wil has to go out earlier sometimes, depending on emergencies and his hospital duties.'

In bed that night, her first night in Kenema, Fiona had her first experience of sleeping under a mosquito net. 'It is like sleeping in a tent,' she laughed as she watched Wil climb under the net before getting into bed. At least they were able to leave the windows open to get the benefit of any breeze – even if it was a hot one.

Wil embraced her and whispered, 'Happy, darling?'

'Of course, deliriously so! Are you?'

'Definitely.'

'Listen to the noises outside! What are they?'

'They're crickets mostly, but some frogs and toads also.'

'Sounds so tropical, doesn't it? Like I've heard in the cinema sometimes.'

'But it is tropical. You are in the tropics now. I think we're only about ten degrees north of the equator you know.'

'No wonder it's so hot. Is it always as hot as this?'

'Yes, it's always hot and humid, but it can get cooler in the rainy season, especially August. It can rain for days then without stopping. That's when most folk get malaria fever. I'd better bring a bottle of mepacrine tablets home for you tomorrow. You'll have to take a couple a day to prevent you catching malaria.'

'Do you take them?'

'No, I don't. Not unless I get a fever. I think I've got a built-in resistance, but you won't have. Hush! Do you hear that buzzing?'

'Yes.'

'That's a mosquito hanging around outside the net. If there's a hole in it, be sure he'll find it.'

Fiona clung to Wil. She felt so good being close to him.

Breakfast next morning, as in most households, was quickly over and by nine o'clock Fiona found herself alone in these unfamiliar surroundings. She busied herself in the morning unpacking what belongings she had been able to include in the forty-four pounds weight restriction on the plane. The furniture in the bedroom was sparse, with only the essentials – the bed, a tallboy and a wardrobe. The adjoining bathroom would have to be shared with Regina's family when they came, but until then it was exclusively theirs. She wandered through the house to familiarise herself with her surroundings, then she ventured outside.

The main dwelling consisted of a large L-shaped, whitewashed bungalow. The front of the house comprised of one large reception room which served as the living room-cum-dining room and led onto a spacious veranda. Off the living room were four bedrooms and two bathrooms. The kitchen was a building apart, connected to the main building by a covered path. Dotted behind the house were all the servants' living quarters. In all, there were eight little mud huts with traditional thatched roofs. This compound nestled in the tropical forest at the foothills of the Kambui hills north of Kenema and was surrounded by trees and dense undergrowth. The civilised world of home and college was literally thousands of miles away and Fiona marvelled at the simplicity of life on the compound. Essentials which she had taken for granted all her life were suddenly distant memories.

Shortly after venturing out a group of black women and children who were round the native huts, drew closer to her. They were obviously rather shy but curious. Aruna came from the kitchen when he heard their chatter.

'They have come to greet you, madam,' he managed to explain. Fiona understood this to mean they wanted to meet her. She went over to them, but they shyly backed away and the children started to hide behind the older women and young girls, looking slightly anxious. She realised that they were perhaps frightened of her, not being used to coming in contact with anybody white before.

Around the compound were a few goats and plenty of domestic fowls and some scruffy half-grown chicks, frantically scratching the bare red lateritic soil and pecking furiously in the hope of finding something edible.

The kitchen was Aruna's domain; there he reigned supreme under Mama Nkozi's eagle eyes. Fiona wandered in there, but both Aruna and Saffa were apparently uncomfortable and unnerved whilst she hovered. Also the heat of the black stove, which Saffa was feeding from a pile of sticks and wood stacked in a corner, was suffocating.

'Is this where you cook all the meals?' Fiona asked. She was surprised to see such an old-fashioned stove still in existence – it reminded her of a museum piece.

'Yes, madam,' was Aruna's reply. He was busy kneading dough on a wooden table.

'What are you making?'

'Bread, madam.'

'How often do you make bread?'

'Each day. Not Sunday, madam.'

'Don't we buy bread at the bakery then?'

'Madam?' Aruna clearly did not understand the question.

A conversation between Aruna and Saffa took place in their local tongue. A pregnant silence then followed, so Fiona concluded she had outstayed her welcome and returned to the house. She helped herself to some orange squash and ensured she used the bottled water from the refrigerator. Wil had warned her of the health hazards of drinking untreated water. She must only drink the boiled, filtered water. He had even recommended she use it to clean her teeth.

The houseboy, Kelly, had made the beds, tidied and swept around the house. The floor was concrete and polished red with one or two rush mats scattered around. Kelly had also done the washing which she'd left, as instructed, in the bath. She could see her clothes spread out over some bushes surrounding the compound. Clotheslines and clothes pegs hadn't reached Sierra Leone either, she concluded. Life was going to be so different here. It was like being on an adventure. Everything was new. She had been transported back in time. She'd been taught and read about how people lived years ago, but what would it be like, she thought, if someone like Aruna were suddenly transported to

Britain? What a cultural shock it would be to encounter the western world and its ways.

The three workers, as Fiona mentally referred to Wil, Mama Nkozi and Kissie, returned that lunchtime to find Fiona on the veranda. Wil kissed her enthusiastically.

'What's my girl been up to then?'

She told them of the morning's events.

'Aruna says he makes the bread. Can't you buy it in Kenema?'

'Darling,' he laughed, 'I'll take you round Kenema at the weekend. You're in for a surprise. There's no bakery. You're a long way from civilised Nottingham now, you know. There are some boys who sell bread at the market, but people make their own generally. It's part of a cook's duties to make the bread.'

Fiona slowly started to settle down to her new married life and soon became familiar with the daily routine. She began to recognise the servants. The household fell into a regular routine and the boys became friendlier as she began to be able to understand their Pidgin English. The compound where they lived consisted of a small community of servants and their extended families. She found she had plenty of spare time when Kissie, Wil and Mama Nkozi were out working and she wandered around acquainting herself with her immediate surroundings.

Wil and Kissie were kept busy at the surgery and Wil also had his duties at the Kenema hospital. Mama Nkozi had the shop in Kenema which sold cotton materials and native cloths. Fiona always looked forward to evenings when they were all together and able to discuss the day's events. Evenings were seldom spent alone because of the numerous visitors calling to pay respects, meet Fiona and enjoy drinks before dinner was served. They would all relax on the veranda, the men with their cold beers while the women drank Sprite or Fanta. The only time Fiona felt she had Wil completely to herself was in bed. She was happy though and seemed to be fitting in with Wil's household and the domineering Mama Nkozi and the efficient Kissie. She was pleased to see that Wil was enjoying his work. Once the baby came, she would be much busier she realised. Wil was attentive and loving and obviously very proud of his young pregnant wife.

A couple of months passed and she was by then seven months' pregnant. The baby would be due sometime in early February. In pecking order, Fiona's household position was third, but she didn't mind. She was also the youngest and she had the man of the house as 'hers'. Christmas was only a couple of weeks away and arrangements were being made for Regina and family to come home. Fiona was looking forward to the change when they would all be together. They were also planning a trip to visit some of old Dr Sankoli's relations to pay their respects.

The Sankoli compound was about three miles outside Kenema on the Hangha road. Fiona had only been into the town once or twice. Aruna went weekly to do the shopping at the Cold Store, the main fresh and frozen food shop. Syrians, Lebanese and Indian traders, ran the only other shops of any interest. There was Chellerams, Choitrams and Chanrais. Fiona had been to them but had been somewhat intimidated by their selling and bargaining tactics. Their eagerness to sell their goods was akin to what she imagined an oriental bazaar must be like. There were no dress shops, no sweet shops, and no bakeries. In fact, most of the shops were equivalent to market stalls and they only sold the bare essentials. Luxury goods, even on a limited scale, were only available from the capital, Freetown.

The days were constantly hot and humid. There had been no rain now for weeks and the red soil was drying out. She often walked around the compound to see the women and children. By now they were no longer afraid of her. She was unable to communicate with them as they only spoke the local Mende or Temeni, the most common of the many local languages. She would sometimes sit outside, sunning herself and watch them working. She soon discovered that the women did the manual work such as gathering and carrying the wood for the fires from the forest around. The size of some of the bundles of wood they could balance and carry on their heads amazed her. The women also worked the ground and tended the crops. She was fascinated by their hairstyles and how they created them. They would sit for hours doing each other's hair in intricate patterns and using black thread to wind round their black frizzy hair to straighten it out. Most of the women around the house only wore a lappa which covered them from the waist to ankles, with no top. Their culture required legs to be covered, but bare breasts were of no interest.

Strange, she thought, how in the west we have come to label bare breasts as a sexual, rather than a purely functional, part of the female body. Yet, by comparison, showing legs and wearing shorts was acceptable in most western countries; such dress would be totally unacceptable in the local African native culture.

The small boys herded the goats and cows. Only men and youths were employed as household servants it seemed.

Most of Fiona's clothes no longer fitted her, apart from some skirts which had to be worn unzipped. There was nowhere to buy maternity clothes. Mama Nkozi and Kissie had all their native costumes made by one of the local tailors.

'I'm sure I could manage to make some dresses if I'd a sewing machine,' Fiona told Kissie one evening while they were chatting on the veranda.

'I think Mama Nkozi has an old sewing machine at the back of the shop. I'll ask her.'

Next day Lansana came home mid-morning to deliver the sewing machine. Kissie hadn't forgotten. It was an old black manual Singer machine. She set about cleaning it straight away and with a bit of oil it worked. That very afternoon Lansana collected her from the house and drove her down to Mama Nkozi's shop where she chose three lengths of cotton material. She carefully unpicked the bodice of one of her old dresses to give her a pattern to work from. So began Fiona's attempts at dressmaking. Clothes didn't last long in any case because of the pounding they were subjected to during the washing process. Kelly literally pounded them on a concrete slab under the running cold-water tap outside. They were rubbed with long cream-coloured bars of soap and pounded like lumps of dough. Mama Nkozi was always complaining about the amount of soap and vim the boys used! After that they faded rapidly from the bleaching effects of being left in the hot sun.

Christmas was nearing, but there was none of the December build-up that preceded it in Britain. The weather was too hot for a start, and Fiona couldn't quite associate Christmas time with hot weather. It always meant cold, dark, bleak weather, sometimes even snow. The shop windows were always decorated and shone brightly in the dark. The children at school always added to the build-up with their excitement, singing carols and eagerly anticipating the arrival of Santa Claus.

Fiona had managed to purchase a few cards from the bookshop and sent them to Judith, Margaret and Sue with letters giving them news of her new life. She also wrote a card to her parents saying she was well and happy and sent love to them. She had still never heard from them since she wrote and told them she was married. This rift with her family did not really trouble her seriously. She would have wished for her parents' approval and blessing and their acceptance of her marriage to Wil. However, she was so happy with him that her state of bliss extended to considering it just a matter of time before her mother would come to realise the error of her judgement. Besides, as long as there was no communication from home, there was no aggravation or unpleasant feelings being aired and Fiona, in her young, rather naïve, view of life began to take this as a period which was moving in the direction of reconciliation. Little did she realise that her mother was in fact nursing her resentment and feeling very much the injured party to what she saw as Fiona's impetuous and wilful behaviour.

Back home, enquiries concerning Fiona's progress and whereabouts were greeted by curtness. Fiona was thought to be working out in Africa on a voluntary teaching assignment which was evidently against her mother's wishes or approval. People soon stopped enquiring when they realised the negative vibes of the situation. Archie, Fiona's father, avoided the subject as far as possible with his wife – anything for a quiet life was his motto, and silence provoked no unpleasant scenes. Stanley was a bit more daring and did at times wonder out loud how Fee was getting on, but in time, he too realised silence was the easiest option.

Jessie, Fiona's mother, was secretly devastated and heartbroken and unfortunately she bore these feelings inwardly, showing only an outward resentment and disapproval. Perhaps deep down she couldn't admit to herself that Fiona had actually grown up, got married and had left the family nest. Of course, she'd always hoped Fiona, and Stanley also, would get married, be happy and settle down to family lives of their own, but with local partners. To go off with a foreigner, and a black one at that, was akin to a family scandal. Some families seemed to be able to cope with scandals of unsuitable marriages, illegitimate births and even criminal events, but not Jessie. She could never handle or admit to anything out of the ordinary regarding her children. As far as she was concerned, Fiona no longer existed. Although she often wondered to herself what was Fiona doing and if was she happy, she tried to blot out all these thoughts and fill their place with hatred. That way, she seemed to handle the situation best. It gave her the strength to overcome any chink of weakness which occasionally dared to show through. When Fiona's first communication from Africa came, in the form of the Christmas card, it was ceremoniously placed on the mantelpiece above the fire with all the rest of the cards. All three of them secretly examined it and read the message, without comment. All of them were pleased to receive the card, though none of them openly admitted so. Stanley knew better than to pass any humorous comment about mud huts and the jungle. His sense of humour would definitely not be appreciated! He would have loved to have a bit more information from Fee though. To him, who had never travelled away from the fishing environment of the North Sea and the Atlantic, what life held in England, let alone Sierra Leone, was an unknown quantity. He wondered when, or even if, they would ever see dear Fee again. He couldn't imagine his mother softening.

Chapter Eight

Two days before Christmas, on the Friday, Regina, Brima and the three children, Poppy, Priscilla and Lahai arrived. Regina's bedroom was already prepared. Priscilla would sleep in Mama Nkozi's bedroom with her, where an extra bed had been set up, Lahai would sleep with his parents and Poppy would share with Kissie, her mother. There was quite an air of excitement around the compound because of the arrival of the family and the start of the holiday period. Many of the servants would make journeys home to visit their families over the Christmas period. Although the servants weren't Christians, the Christmas tradition was recognised because Sierra Leone was one of the British Colonies and as such had adopted the Christian holidays. That Friday evening heralded the start of a four-day long festival of constant activity, partying and feasting. The house was open to streams of calling visitors and relations.

It was about three o'clock when the car arrived from Freetown. They had travelled all day and were tired and weary, but the excitement kept their energy flowing. At least they had arrived while it was still daylight. The three children seemed to be everywhere at once. This was the first time they had met Fiona and were obviously a bit overawed by her. Like the servants, they were not accustomed to seeing, let alone being close to, a white person, so they were shy and awkward with her initially.

They stayed up late that night. After the children eventually settled down they sat out on the veranda to catch the warm breeze coming down from the hills behind, drank and talked excitedly. Regina and Brima wanted to know all about family and friends and catch up on events since their last visit. Much of the conversation meant little to Fiona. They spoke a little too fast for her to comprehend fully, also they were discussing people Fiona didn't yet know or hadn't met. She enjoyed that evening, though on the sidelines, of this obviously happy, family reunion. Of course there were some tears shed and sadness as this was the first time Regina had been back since Papa's death and his memory was still very fresh in all their thoughts. The family, together again, drew attention to his absence; this would be their first Christmas without him.

Regina was anxious to know how Fiona was finding life and what she missed most since leaving her home. Fiona felt sorry that Regina lived so far away. She could feel closer to her than either Mama Nkozi or Kissie. Somehow Kissie had an air of independent superiority about her which didn't encourage intimacy between them. With Regina, she felt much more relaxed and friendly.

Wil and Brima talked together at length. It was good to see them together, another male to share the house with. Although Wil had several male friends calling socially, he was after all, outnumbered one to three at home. It was after one o'clock before they all retired.

The bedroom was the only place that Fiona was alone with Wil, so she cherished the few hours they spent there alone. They often spent hours lying in bed together before falling asleep. These were the times that Fiona looked forward to, when he was completely hers. She had to compete with his long working hours and the family for his attention. Their togetherness held a special magic for her. Feeling his skin, even the touch of his hand in hers, brought an overpowering sense of belonging. The hot nights meant they weren't inhibited with clothes or blankets. They could lie together, their bodies entwined throughout the night, covered only with a cotton sheet. Their lovemaking was an expression of their commitment to each other. They were both looking forward to the baby's arrival to seal and prove their love for each other. She knew intuitively that he was happy. He was undoubtedly enjoying his work and it was fulfilling a deep-seated desire to give back to his country some of the privileges he had had the good fortune to enjoy. She knew that Wil considered with some disappointment that too many of the professional Sierra Leoneans turned their back on their poorer countrymen and chose to practise abroad and enjoy the fruits of the civilised world.

'That's human nature though,' Fiona had pointed out.

'Yes, I suppose it is and I can't blame them for that, but I feel an obligation to repay something,' he'd replied.

Obviously he'd made the right decision for himself. He was settling down to life and work at home much sooner than she'd anticipated. After all, he'd lived and worked in England, apart from his annual trips home, for seventeen years, since he was fifteen years old, more than half his life. He was already gaining considerable respect and popularity in the community.

Christmas Day, like every other day, was hot. The weather wasn't variable like British weather and didn't merit the in-depth analysis that the British tended to give theirs. She would soon discover that every day was hot and humid, with the addition that during the rainy season it was also very wet. The skies on that day were hazy and a hot, dry wind was blowing gently from the north.

'It's Harmattan weather again,' Mama Nkozi informed her.

'What's that?'

'It's the wind blowing south from the Sahara desert. That's why it's so dry. We get it every December and January time. You'll hear the furniture cracking sometimes. It dries out the wood and shrinks it. The table will crack open down this join here soon and then it closes up again when the more humid weather returns with the onset of the rains. It happens every year. '

Christmas Day was perfect. Two goats were barbecued on a spit outside with several chickens. Aruna, Saffa and Kelly had slaughtered the animals and prepared them. Fiona was uneasy about eating the goat meat. She furtively looked around the compound for the little herd of goats which was always grazing nearby, trying to see if she could identify which ones were slowly roasting on the spit. She hoped it wasn't her favourite little black and tan one with the huge brown trusting eyes. She called him Billyboy. She definitely couldn't bring herself to eat little Billyboy, she thought. No, thank goodness, she realised he was still grazing unsuspectingly a few feet away.

Food was provided for all the servants and their families. Pots of rice were cooking over the open fires and dried fish was available. All the women and children were dressed magnificently in their best costumes. Palm wine flowed freely for the men servants.

That first tropical Christmas Day was such fun for her! She couldn't imagine anything so completely different from her past Christmases. In fact, she couldn't really believe it was Christmas. There had been no visit of Santa Claus for the children and no exchanging of gifts between them. Instead it was a day of feasting in the open with everybody in the compound. There was no turkey, Brussel sprouts, mince pies or Christmas pudding. She was as far from home culturally that day as she was in distance. The day drew to a close too quickly for her.

Dusk was practically non-existent due to the closeness of the equator. It only took about ten minutes for the sun to set and daylight to turn to darkness.

'If only we could have the long, light summer nights that we get in Britain,' she lamented. 'It's dark here every night around six o'clock.'

'You can't have everything in life you want, my darling,' Wil had pointed out to her. 'You forget we don't have the snow and the cold here, so that has to make up for the long hours of daylight in the summer that you miss. You can't have it all ways you know!'

That evening they all relaxed on the veranda as usual. Friends steadily came and went extending their greetings. The family were all tired from overeating, but pleasantly so. Celebrations continued late into the night on the compound. The servants were partying, full of good food and intoxicated from the local palm wine. A wind-up record player was playing well-scratched 78 rpm records, drums were beating, and singing and dancing was in full swing.

'Come, let's walk down to the end of the road, darling. I could do with the exercise. I'm so full with overeating,' Wil requested.

'Fine, I'll go and get the torch and a stick.'

Together they strolled out into the night arm-in-arm, Wil shining the torch on the laterite path ahead to alert any snakes basking in the heat of the dirt road, while Fiona scraped the stick alongside her to make some noise, also to warn unsuspecting snakes of their approach. Snakes were common in and around the compound, but provided they were not caught by surprise, they would slither quickly out of the way into the nearest ground cover.

'Enjoy your first African Christmas then?'

'Yes, it's been such a super day, hasn't it? Everybody seems to have enjoyed themselves, don't you think?'

'Everything's gone off well. Even Mama enjoyed it. I expect it's been a difficult year without Papa.'

'You being at home with her must have a lot to do with that. She must be so happy now that you're home again taking over his work and the family responsibilities. That must go a long way to help compensate for his death.'

'I think she's looking forward to the baby coming also. It's hard on her that Regina and her kids are in Freetown. She'd like them nearer I suppose.'

'Don't I know that! It seems that all mothers want their daughters at home with them.'

'Sorry, sweetheart, I didn't mean that. Do you miss home? Do you feel homesick at all?'

'No, silly, of course I don't. Just funny that mothers everywhere are basically the same. Can't bear to see their kids leave home.'

'I love you, darling.'

'And I love you too,' she whispered back.

They walked the half-mile down to the main road and turned back towards the house. Crickets were chirping loudly all round. The black sky was splattered with hundreds of stars. The rhythm of the drums and the chanting of the natives as they sang and danced interrupted the stillness of the evening. Something in the atmosphere coupled with the warmth gave her the sensation of being on holiday on some tropical island. It seemed incredible that this was now her home. They turned the bend on the road and could see the veranda light in the distance. They slowly strolled towards the veranda steps. The halo of the veranda light, as usual, was attracting masses of moths and insects vying frantically with each other to get closer to the bulb. She was slowly learning to cope with the unfamiliar winged and crawling insects and accept them as a way of life. Her biggest hatred was the huge dark brown cockroaches with their two long front feelers which scuttled around at night. Kelly would stamp down on them with his bare feet and the crushing noise as he squashed them to death always made her feel quite squeamish. They were lucky to have electric lights. The little generator they had chugged away to provide the house and kitchen with lights, even though they were very dim by European standards. The refrigerator wasn't powered by the electric generator; instead it was run off a kerosene tank. Powering a refrigerator, or any electrical device, would have put too much strain on the generator, which was used solely for lighting the living quarters. The generator was also a temperamental machine and broke down often, so the kerosene-run refrigerator was much more reliable. The unit worked like the Tilley lamps Fiona had seen in remote Scottish crofts. The wick had to be carefully trimmed like the wicks on lamps, otherwise the unit emitted a spiral of black smoke.

They climbed the four steps up to join the others on the veranda. 'I'll just go and get a beer and then have a wander round the back to see how the celebrations are coming on,' Wil said to Brima. 'Do you want to come as well?'

'Bring me out a Heineken as well while you're there,' Brima called to Wil as he went towards the fridge. 'I'll come along. I think it'll be a good idea to show our faces. Why don't we all stroll over for half an hour or so? It's only nine o'clock now.'

Oil lamps and the burning embers of a few fires outside the huts provided light. People energetically dancing to a combination of drums and the old wind-up gramophone were having a high time. Everybody seemed to be taking part. Even the children and the elderly were keeping up with the rigorous body movements and intricate footwork required. Nobody needed a partner it seemed. Mama Nkozi took off into the group of dancers, shuffling her feet on the dry dusty soil, wiggling her huge body in time with the rhythm, to the clapping and cheering of the dancers. Soon, they were all joining in. Fiona was initially unwilling to have a go, but Kelly appeared and insisted she copy his simple footwork and in no time she was mastering the basics and shuffling around in time to the beat. The body movements were impossible though – they simply didn't come naturally to her. Everybody seemed to be enjoying themselves and the dancing went on and on. The half hour extended to two hours, then exhausted and choking with the rising dust, they all stumbled back to the house. Their feet and legs were covered in the red lateritic dust which had been stirred up from the dry ground as they shuffled and twisted around.

'What fun that was!' exclaimed Fiona. 'They are certainly enjoying themselves down there tonight!'

'They've always got plenty energy for singing and dancing. I wish they would work as hard as they danced,' Kissie replied with some asperity. 'Old Aruna won't be much fun tomorrow when he's nursing a gross hangover after all that palm wine.'

Fiona was beginning to think that Kissie was a bit too harsh with the servants, but she decided, as it was Christmas Day she wouldn't make an issue of her comment. Instead she said, 'I'm going to give my feet and legs a wash and then I'm off to bed. I'm feeling the worse for all this extra weight I'm carrying around. Goodnight everybody! See you all in the morning.' And so ended Fiona's first tropical Christmas.

On the Wednesday following Christmas Day the whole family took an outing to visit relations of Mama Nkozi and her late husband. This was Fiona's first visit away from Kenema so she was looking forward to the trip. They set off straight after breakfast in two cars on the two-hour journey which took them just past Kailahun, very close to the Liberian border. The three children had been very little trouble since their arrival. They had been spending most of their time playing outside and mixing with the children on the compound.

At breakfast that particular Wednesday, arrangements were being made concerning travelling. Wil said he would drive so that Lansana would have the day off and Brima would take a car as well.

'I'll travel with Brima and Regina,' Fiona volunteered. She was enjoying Regina's company and that meant there would be three adults in each car if Mama Nkozi, Kissie and Wil travelled together.

'Can I come with you, Auntie Fiona?' Priscilla asked.

'Of course you can. You can sit in the back with me and your mama can sit in front.'

'I'll take Lahai on my knee. He'll have to come with me. He'll be too much trouble otherwise,' said Regina.

'Can I come in your car, papa?' Poppy asked Wil.

Kissie immediately said, 'Yes, you must come and keep your mama company. I've hardly seen you so far these holidays, there's been so much happening.'

Fiona felt a little sorry for Poppy then. Up until then she hadn't really given any thought to who was Poppy's father and how Kissie was bringing her up on her own. The family were very supportive and Kissie was effectively one of the Sankoli family. During school terms Regina and Brima were really bringing her up as a part of their family, but deep down the child obviously needed a father so presumably she considered Wil as her father figure.

The dirt road was bordered on both sides by dense vegetation which was heavily powdered with the red dust which billowed out behind every passing vehicle. Travelling was extremely unpleasant. The heat necessitated open windows to catch some moving air. Then the clouds of dust in the wake of passing vehicles covered everything and everybody in the car. Wil had set off about five minutes earlier than Brima so that the second vehicle would not be travelling continuously in Wil's dust trail. Most of the passing vehicles were mammy wagons displaying brightly painted slogans on them like 'That's my boy!' or 'Better late than the late!'. Brima was explaining to Fiona that these mammy wagons were the equivalent of busses and taxis. They were lorries, or cattle wagons, as Fiona knew them, and the passengers paid the driver and were transported to their destination along the main routes in the back of the truck. Passengers were usually accompanied by heavy bundles of luggage and even livestock, such as sheep, goats and chickens. They all shared the available space on the back of the lorry. These mammy wagons were the natives' only means of getting to most of the villages in the interior.

Driving was a hazardous undertaking on the single-track roads. Although wide enough for two vehicles, the wheels over time, particularly during the wet season, formed distinct furrows down the centre of the road, separated by a central ridge, high enough to catch many a car sump. Consequently driving down the centre of the road was the only way to travel. Fortunately the roads were not particularly busy, but a battle of wills usually ensued when an approaching mammy wagon driver would hold his ground and refuse to pull off the single track to the left side, forcing the car driver to take evasive action into the dust-laden shrubbery to avoid a head-on collision. It was a situation like the American game of chicken. The larger vehicle invariably won!

Ruts and potholes in the road were commonplace and to add to the unpleasantness of the dust clouds, corrugations had formed on the compacted laterite, making the car shudder continuously. Fiona began to feel she was travelling on a pneumatic drill.

'Thank goodness we have tar roads in Freetown,' remarked Regina. 'Our car wouldn't stand up to too much of this treatment.'

'The dust has got all up my nose as well,' complained Fiona. 'Thank goodness I'm wearing these sunglasses. At least they help to keep the dust out of my eyes. You know I'm sweating so much my underwear is wet!'

'Don't worry, we'll soon be there,' Brima added. 'I would guess about fifteen minutes more or so.'

They turned off the main track onto a side road about the same width as the road leading to their own compound. The grass was still growing in the central ramp, indicating that few vehicles used the path. They approached a clearing with mud houses on both sides, set back from the track. Several of the houses were used as small shops with their few articles for sale neatly laid out in front of the dwellings. Fiona noticed that the wares usually comprised cigarettes, matches, soap and foodstuffs like rice, tinned pilchards, dried fish and sometimes oranges and bananas. The bare sandy ground around the huts was neatly swept. The inhabitants of these huts soon appeared with inquisitive children to wave at the car and its occupants as they drove slowly past. Before they reached the end of the huts they swung left into an area behind the main through track and there Fiona saw Wil's car parked outside a much larger dwelling with an elaborate veranda with a wooden railing around it. As soon as the car stopped, and even before the engine was switched off, it was completely surrounded by about a dozen highly excited relations, all strangers to Fiona. It reminded her of her arrival at Kenema airport. Introductions followed, and Wil carefully guided Fiona round everybody. This was the home of his uncle, his father's brother and their extended family. Also present were members of Mama Nkozi's close family, including her old mother. She was a frail old lady, small and wizened, but quite alert. Members of the extended family arrived throughout the day to greet them and pay their respects. It transpired that most of the people living in this little settlement formed part of their family. Relationships and families in Sierra Leone were very important. Family groups worked and lived together, with the elderly being taken care of by the rest of the family and community.

'This sort of relationship has long since fallen away in Britain,' Fiona sadly told Wil's elderly grandmother. Wil had to translate as the old lady spoke no English. She held Fiona's hands between her two small palms and told Wil how happy she was to live long enough to see so many of her family surrounding her and how proud she was of them all. She also was happy to see Fiona 'got belly' which was a good sign of her fertility. She was nearing eighty years old, which was quite a record by Sierra Leonean standards. Wil had already told Fiona that the life expectancy of the average native was only forty-two, the lowest in the world. Grandmother had given birth to fifteen children altogether, five having died before the age of one year. Only three of these children, which included Mama Nkozi, were now alive, so the old woman had experienced much sorrow during her lifetime.

Fiona gravitated towards Regina eventually. Wil was continually engaged in conversation with different relations. Regina confided in Fiona that these visits were an essential part of family life and the elderly had to be shown respect by the younger members of the family. Fiona had certainly noticed that even the very young children were respectful of all the elderly. It was part of the traditional upbringing. She had noticed, however, that the youngsters accorded little respect for the servants. This she found distasteful. She had several times overheard Poppy and Priscilla ordering the servants around and unfortunately they humbly obeyed. Fiona had mentioned this to Wil, who had told her that this was quite acceptable. There wasn't equality amongst fellow

Sierra Leoneans. The tribal system which formed the country's culture was not democratic.

The house was packed and several conversations were going on. The men had gathered together and were drinking vast quantities of bottled beer. The women were provided with a constant supply of warmish tinned soft drinks. Fiona was very much the centre of attention. No one in the family had ever married someone white so she was treated rather like a celebrity.

Round about two o'clock a vast amount of food was carried onto a couple of rush mats in the centre of the room and everybody ate in a communal fashion using their hands. Fiona found this quite difficult, especially when it came to the rice. Regina helped and gave her demonstrations on how to take the rice and neatly roll it up into a ball in her right hand. Some of the sauces were very hot, bringing tears to Fiona's eyes and caused sweat to drip from her face. The children were taking handfuls of food outside to eat and were having much fun being chased by the domestic fowls eager to peck up the morsels which were dropping onto the ground. What a bizarre party this was. She wished that Wil had given her some prior advice on how to integrate with these people beforehand. She was particularly conscious of being watched and didn't want to make any cultural gaffs if possible.

Priscilla started to wedge herself between Regina and Fiona.

'Mama, I need to go to the latrine.'

'I'll come with you just now,' was Regina's response.

'I'll take her if you like. I want to go as well,' Fiona interrupted.

'Fine then. Out the back to your right.'

The two of them went outside in search of the toilet but Fiona couldn't find it. Then Priscilla said, 'It's in here,' as she entered a small round thatched mud hut with an opening for a doorway. It had no windows.

'No, dear, I don't think so,' Fiona said to her as she bent down to enter the opening, only to find the hut empty.

'Yes, it is,' Priscilla said as she started pulling her pants down and off. She squatted down and wet onto the dusty floor. 'I have to take my panties off in case I wet on them,' she confided in Fiona. 'You can do it next to me.'

The doorway was now crowded with about half a dozen children just standing and watching Fiona.

'No, I don't think I need to go any more,' Fiona said and retreated to the house embarrassed.

Once next to Regina, she said, 'Have you been to the toilet outside yet?'

'Not yet.' Then she looked at her and started to laugh.

'Are you sure that is the toilet?'

'Yes, I'm sure. You've never been to the bush toilet before have you?' Her laughter was infectious and Fiona started to giggle.

'Won't you come with me? All the kids were standing at the door watching me, and also what if one of the men should come in?'

'Come with me now.'

They went outside to the little hut together. The children started to move towards the open door again but Regina sent them scurrying.

'Don't worry. I'll stand here by the door and you can go inside.'

Fiona squatted, like Priscilla had done, and watched the stream of urine splash onto the dirt floor and flow away from her. Her thoughts at the time were relief that she only needed to urinate! She wondered what happened otherwise. She could only guess that one of the servants had to ensure that this latrine was kept supplied with clean dry sand. Thank goodness they had septic tanks on the compound at home! She then remembered the time she'd been on a school trip to Paris and her confusion in the public toilets there. She remembered how much amusement that system had caused amongst her and her school friends at the time.

Darkness had fallen by the time they prepared to leave. Oil lamps were lit. There was no electricity in the village. After a lengthy round of farewells, they set off for the long, uncomfortable drive back home. However in the cooler evening air, without the brilliant sunshine, the return journey was not so exhausting.

The week between Christmas and New Year passed so quickly. Fiona enjoyed all the company and activity. Afterwards Regina and family returned to Freetown but Poppy remained. She would stay until it was time to return to school.

The household returned to normal with Wil, Kissie and Mama Nkozi returning to work. Fiona had Poppy for company. She was seven and a well-mannered, quiet girl. She warmed to the attention Fiona gave her. Fiona thought she was a neglected, undemanding little soul and after those two weeks they had become firm friends.

'Next time you come, we'll have the new baby to look after,' Fiona told her.

'Will you still be my special friend when you've got the baby as well?' she asked.

'Of course, I'll always be your special friend,' Fiona assured her. 'You'll just have to help me look after the baby.'

'I can do that easily. I sometimes look after Lahai now when Auntie Regina is busy. I want to be a nurse like Mama when I'm big. Then I'll be able to look after lots of babies.'

'Do you really want to be a nurse when you're big?'

'Yes, but Papa says I should be a doctor like him, but Mama says I would have to go to England to learn to be a doctor and I don't want to leave my Mama and Auntie Regina behind.'

Fiona had noticed that Poppy was calling Wil 'Papa' quite often now. She'd originally thought nothing about it, but now she was beginning to wonder who was Poppy's father. None of the family had ever referred to him and Fiona hadn't really given the matter any consideration. She didn't really want to ask Kissie such a personal question. In any case Kissie had never volunteered any information about whether she had been married or not. She wasn't a particularly chatty person, unlike Regina, and Fiona often found her somewhat aloof and evasive. The question now started to niggle away in Fiona's mind. She regretted not having asked Regina. She felt sure Regina would have been able to tell her. She knew that Kissie had been part of the Sankoli household for over ten years now, so she would have had Poppy whilst still working with Wil's father at the surgery.

In bed, the night after Poppy left to return to Freetown and school, Fiona said, 'I missed Poppy today. She was good company when you were all out at work.'

'She's very fond of you. She's not used to getting so much individual attention. I can see you've made a firm little friend there,' was Wil's response.

'Do you know who her father is, darling?'

'Have you asked Kissie?'

'No, I was just wondering. Was she ever married?'

'No, she's never been married. She came to work with my father as soon as she qualified and she's been with us as part of the family ever since.'

'So she was here when she had Poppy?'

'Oh, yes, darling. Having an illegitimate child here isn't quite the scandal it is in Britain, you know.'

'No, I suppose not, it's just that Poppy calls you "Papa" and I wondered why.'

'Well, she used to call my father "Grandpapa" also! You don't mind, do you?'

'No, of course not. It's good to give her a sense of family security.'

'She's just an accepted part of the family now and is always considered as one of us.'

From Wil's casual reaction she assumed that he wasn't really interested in the subject so she didn't pursue the conversation.

Chapter Nine

January was a very hot, less humid, month with the dry Harmattan blowing. Fiona was beginning to feel uncomfortable with the weight of the baby. The heat made it difficult for her to sleep comfortably at night. During the day she kept busy around the house. She'd discovered a cookery book and had managed to work out weights very roughly using tablespoons and teaspoons. The old kitchen stove presented a challenge also, but she did manage some success with cakes, pastry and scones.

At first Aruna stayed aloof from Fiona's culinary attempts. Saffa was however an eager onlooker and begged her to teach him to bake. His ambition was to graduate from 'small boy' and eventually get a cook's position. He was eager to find out the ingredients and quantities used. He was a very friendly uncomplicated boy.

Fiona realised that cook's disapproval and lack of interest stemmed from a fear of her encroaching on what was his territory. He was in charge of the kitchen and resented any interference. After one or two baking sessions encouraged by the others, particularly Mama Nkozi, who thoroughly enjoyed the cake results, she discovered that Aruna had been asking Saffa to tell him the recipes so that he would also know how to bake. Gradually old Aruna softened towards Fiona and her attempts in the kitchen. Perhaps he realised that his job wasn't in jeopardy after all.

Wil had started to play tennis some evenings with a friend, Meynard Harris. Meynard was 'in diamonds' according to Wil and he had a tennis court at his house in Kenema. The exercise and the company was good for him after work. Fiona had been a few times in the evening before sunset with Wil and Kissie to Meynard's house but she couldn't participate in the tennis because of her advanced state of pregnancy. Kissie and Meynard's wife, Kolili, or his oldest son, Lamin, would make up a foursome for doubles. Fiona enjoyed these games of tennis because of the change of environment from their own compound. The short drive and the different company was something to look forward to.

During her last few weeks, Fiona became restless and now was only looking forward to the birth. Wil had arranged for her to have the baby at the hospital in Kenema and one of his colleagues, Dr Roxy Boston, would be on hand for the delivery. She was apprehensive about the whole process, but Mama Nkozi and Kissie had assured her that there was little to worry about.

'Just a necessary discomfort!' Kissie had commented.

The excitement started to rise with the realisation that the birth was imminent sometime at the beginning of February. Regina had sent a parcel of nappies and baby clothes up from Freetown that she no longer needed. Wil had a local carpenter make a cot and it was installed in the bedroom. She found she wasn't comfortable in any position by then and longed for the day when the baby would arrive. It seemed such a long time ago now that Fiona and Judith had realised she was pregnant. A saying of her mother's came to mind – 'so much water has gone under the bridge since then'. That was the first time since Christmas that Fiona thought about her mum and home. Perhaps it was the uncertainty and fear of what the next few weeks would bring that turned her thoughts to home. She wished her mother knew about the baby, but even more she wished her mother could acknowledge and accept Wil as her son-in-law.

Milton Sankoli arrived slightly later than expected, on the 16 February, and weighed in at 8lb 5oz; a large healthy boy. Fiona had to endure a long and difficult labour. The birth process was not as easy as she'd been led to believe. Either that or African women were more suited to having children, she thought to herself rather sourly.

Wil was ecstatic and all the family and servants rejoiced and celebrated long into the night whilst Fiona was too weak and exhausted to participate. She'd only been in hospital for the birth, then Wil took them both straight home. A son's birth seemed to be more important in Sierra Leone than the birth of a daughter. Perhaps this reflected the tradition that women generally had lower status than men. She had noticed various indications of this. Men showed deference to other men in their greetings, but not women. Fiona had also seen that when a man was out walking with his wife, she would be walking quite a distance behind him, and she would be bearing a child on her back as well as a load on her head, whilst he would be walking in front carrying nothing. Wil had explained to her that this was the recognised tribal custom. Women, as wives, were still bought with cattle and it was quite in order to have more than one wife. Some tribal chiefs would have up to four or six wives, she learned, and they would be out working in the fields. It was very prestigious to own several wives and have many children. This was a sign of wealth and status. The fatter the wives, the wealthier the man was assumed to be.

There had been no problem choosing baby Sankoli's name. Before he was born the subject of names had been discussed between the four of them: Wil, Mama Nkozi, Kissie and Fiona. The only name put forward for a son was Milton. This had been old Dr Sankoli's Christian name. Also, that year, 1961, was the year that Sierra Leone was to become independent and Milton Margai would be sworn in as the country's first Prime Minister. So, Milton was the only possible choice! A daughter would have been named Nkozi after Wil's mother. Fiona hadn't really had much opportunity to put forward any of her choices. So Milton it was. They all agreed that Papa would have been so proud of this grandson being named after him had he been alive.

It took Fiona nearly two weeks to get back on her feet again. Kissie was very good with helping to teach her the fundamentals of baby care. She had trouble feeding him herself which meant he was underfed and consequently cried a lot, much to Fiona's distress and frustration. He was crying from hunger and eventually after three weeks she had to resort to bottle-feeding to satisfy the child. The Cold Store Pharmacy sold Cow & Gate baby milk which she changed to and then things improved. Milton started to gain weight steadily and became quite contented and much easier to care for.

Kissie became much more friendly towards Fiona. She clearly loved helping with baby Milton. He was surely bringing out her maternal instincts and probably she was feeling a bit broody was

Fiona's conclusion. At least she was less aloof towards Fiona. Between the four of them he was getting the best possible attention. Fiona had no housework, washing or cooking to attend to so she was free to nurse and dote on him all day. He was good at night and luckily Wil's sleep was seldom disturbed on the odd occasions when he did wake. Wil was by now wholly involved in his work and consequently spent long hours both at the hospital and the surgery.

When Milton was about six weeks, Kissie was tending to him one day after work. Wil had gone to play tennis with Meynard.

'I wish I'd a son like you,' she was telling Milton as she nursed him and he was responding with smiles as if he understood. 'You know there's not nearly so much attention paid to baby girls.' She was now addressing Fiona. Mama Nkozi was bathing at the time so they were alone.

'I'd actually noticed that. I wonder if Wil would have been disappointed if we'd had a daughter instead? He seemed sure right from the day I told him I was pregnant that it would be a boy.'

'Of course he would have been. Look at Poppy. He never paid nearly as much attention to her when she was born. It would have been different if she'd been a boy.'

'But Wil's very fond of her, isn't he? In fact he looks on her as a daughter in a way.'

'Well, and so he should, she is his daughter,' she snapped.

'You mean Poppy is really Wil's child? Is that what you're saying?' gasped Fiona.

'Yes, it's time you knew the truth. They all asked me not to tell you, but I don't think it's fair on me,' she blurted out. 'He should have been my husband, then instead he goes and marries you and now you've given him the most important thing a man wants – a male child.' Then she promptly burst into tears.

Fiona was stunned. She just sat speechless and motionless, rooted to the chair she sat on. Milton began to cry also, being aware of Kissie's distraught state. Fiona leapt over to Kissie and put her arms round her.

'I'm sorry Kissie... I'm so sorry... please don't cry, please,' Fiona pleaded. 'You'll upset me as well as Milton. I'd honestly no idea at all. I really didn't know. Please believe me.'

At that, Kissie passed Milton back into Fiona's arms and fled from the room. Fiona consoled him and he soon rallied. She took him out into the kitchen and asked Saffa to amuse him for a little while, then she went back inside to look for Kissie. She'd retreated to her bedroom, but Fiona went in after her and sat on the bed with her. She'd stopped crying but looked so downcast and unhappy.

'Please tell me about it, Kissie, please. I'm not your enemy. I want to be your friend and help,' Fiona pleaded. She really didn't know how to handle the situation.

'There's not much you can do now, is there? He was meant for me and you got him.'

'Just explain it all to me. You must realise I'm an innocent party to all this.'

'There's not much to explain. You see my family and Wil's family had always planned that I would marry Wil. It's local tradition that the family agrees on a suitable match. I came and joined this family and worked with old Dr. Sankoli as soon as I qualified, then Wil was always considered mine. When he used to come home on his holidays he always belonged to me. It's quite normal for us to have children before a wedding takes place. I always thought that we would get married as soon as he came back to join his Papa in the practice. Then when he does come back he tells us he's married you. By tribal law I'm also his wife, but he doesn't come to me any more since you've been here.'

'At least I know the truth now. You know I did wonder who Poppy's father was and I did ask Wil one night but he was evasive and implied she was illegitimate, so I didn't think any more about it.'

'I don't know how he thought he'd keep it a secret from you. Everybody knows he's her father.'

'I'm glad you've told me yourself, Kissie. I was going to ask Regina next time I saw her and it's better I hear it from you than from her. Mind, I would have preferred if Wil had told me himself.'

'I'll go and bath and change now I think.'

'Do you feel better now? Do you think this has cleared the air between you and me?'

'I suppose it has, but remember I'll always want Wil, I can't deny that.'

Fiona was perturbed by her remark, but ignored it by asking, 'If you bath now, will you see to Milton when you're changed so that I can bath before dinner?'

'Yes, of course I will,' was her reply.

Fiona didn't know what to think or do. She went and got Milton from Saffa and when Kissie returned to the room, she went to run her bath water. Normally she waited until Wil came home to bath so they could share the water to save wastage. The water came from a spring high up in the hills behind them. Cold water was piped to the kitchen and the two bathrooms but the only hot water available to the two baths was heated in a forty-gallon drum outside. Kelly had to light a fire under the drum daily to provide the heat for the water, then it was piped to the two baths. It was a very basic system, but it worked quite efficiently. The hot water was always a rusty colour from the inside of the drum though.

She sat in the bath numbed. Why hadn't Wil told her? How long had he hoped to keep it a secret? She'd given him the ideal opportunity when she'd broached the subject and he'd chosen not to respond. From what Kissie said, everybody would know that Kissie had been his unofficial wife. She wondered how they saw her position. Every day they worked together down at the surgery. They got on well, maybe even better than well. Yet Kissie had been upset because he no longer came to her. Presumably she meant that they were no longer sexual partners. At least that was reassuring to know. She felt like crying, but tears wouldn't come and in any case what good would crying do? Then she felt angry that she'd been deceived. It seemed like her world had somehow exploded around her. The water was starting to cool and darkness had fallen when she heard Wil's car arrive.

'I see you're already in the bath are you, darling,' he called out to her through the door separating the bathroom and bedroom.

'I'm just getting out though. The water's not all that hot, you'd better get in right away.'

'Fine, I'll do that. How's things today? I've seen Milton and he's starting to doze off. I told Kissie to take him through to bed.'

'Fine, darling,' Fiona replied automatically. 'How was your day? Did you have a good game with Meynard?'

'Yes, but I'm finding it more and more difficult to beat young Lamin.'

'Well, he gets a lot more practice than you do and also he hasn't done a day's work like you.'

'Give me a kiss then,' he asked as he passed her in the bathroom.

Fiona already had a towel round her as Wil stepped into the water.

'You all right?'

'Yes, why?'

'I just wondered. You seemed quiet.'

'No, I'm just fine,' she replied curtly.

Fiona was still very shocked, even though half a suspicion had occasionally crept into her thoughts. She wasn't sure how to tackle Wil about this. She decided to mull it over as long as she could. She didn't want to cause unpleasantness amongst the four of them. The trouble with sharing the house meant that she had to be careful not to draw Kissie and Mama Nkozi into any disagreement she had with Wil. She couldn't be sure how Wil would react and she felt she couldn't cope with any kind of disharmony. Kissie obviously harboured a deep grudge against her. She'd managed to contain it, but now with Milton's arrival and all the attention he was attracting, Kissie's maternal instincts had surfaced in a growing jealousy and resentment of her position within the family.

The evening passed quite uneventfully, as it often did. They ate dinner and relaxed over coffee and had no callers for after-dinner drinks. Kissie had composed herself well and carried on the usual discussions with Wil about some of the patients they'd treated during the course of the day. Fiona knew quite a lot about what went on at the surgery through these discussions. Mama Nkozi also got involved in the discussions and although she had her own business, she liked to keep abreast of what went on especially now that Wil was in charge and still new to the practice.

Most of the patients they treated at the surgery were seriously ill from what Fiona could gather. Wil often complained that they only came to him as a last resort, when the work of the witch doctors had failed. It was difficult to gain the confidence of the natives. They held a deep suspicion of modern medicines, preferring instead to believe in the power of ancient spirits and the healing powers of the witch doctors. The Sierra Leoneans were still very primitive people. Altogether there were about eighteen ethnic groups which comprised the total population of the small country, their culture was based on tradition and superstition and they played an important role in their upbringing and beliefs. The village chiefs wielded considerable power and they had jurisdiction over most domestic disputes.

Other powerful bodies were the secret societies. Young boys and girls underwent initiation as they approached adulthood. These secret societies, Poro for the boys and Bundu for the girls, trained them over many months in tribal culture, crafts and law. These secret societies had their own devils that danced on special occasions.

It was difficult to find out what exactly went on, but Wil used to become angry at the barbarous methods employed on the young girls when removing their clitoris. This was done to ensure fidelity in marriage and the operations were performed by women using glass or old razor blades without any form of anaesthetic. He realised that the tradition would continue, but he would have preferred it to be carried out under sterile conditions so that the risk of blood poisoning and haemorrhage was minimised. It was not uncommon for girls to die as a result of these operations and on a few occasions he had been asked to treat girls after complications had arisen and had been unable to save their lives. His father had dealt with many such cases and he had always maintained that without education and pressure from civilised society to change this tradition, these ceremonies would continue.

That night Fiona listened to the familiar chatter which revolved round that day's surgery. The rains would be starting soon and with their onset the usual increase in malaria patients.

Fiona had only half of her attention on the conversation. Her thoughts were still confused. She thought perhaps the only way to solve the problem was by being forthright and without emotional drama. She must keep her cool and discuss it openly. As soon as they got into bed, Fiona asked Wil to leave the light on.

'Why, darling?'

'Because I want to speak to you. I've got something rather important to say.'

'This sounds ominous.'

'Yes, you could say that. It's about Poppy. Why couldn't you have been honest with me and told me that you are her father?'

'Who told you that?'

'Is it really important how I found out? Don't you think it was your duty to tell me, particularly when I asked you at Christmas. It now seems that you cleverly avoided the issue then.'

'Now, listen to me, darling.'

'Don't darling me. I want the truth. Please give me an honest answer.' Suddenly Fiona felt she was losing control, so she took a deep breath. Keep calm now and don't antagonise him. Give him a chance to have his say, she thought to herself.

'Please, Wil, just tell me.'

'Do we have to go through this now? Can't it wait? I'm really tired. It's been a busy day.'

'Please yourself, but I would like you to give me some explanation. Did you think I wouldn't find out? Were you deliberately deceiving me?'

'Please, Fiona, look at it from my point of view.'

'Until you give me your point of view, I'll find that rather difficult.'

'Yes, I suppose so.'

He put his arms round her and gently kissed her.

'I'm waiting,' was her frosty response.

'Let's put the light out, tuck the mosquito net in and settle down first. Please understand,' he said, 'I never wanted to deceive you. I only wanted to avoid a situation like we've got now, where you've found out and are cross and upset with me. I knew there was something up with you tonight when I got home. I always know when you go silent on me, something's not quite right.

'Up until I met you it was always assumed I'd come back home and work and I'd settle down with Kissie. Our families had agreed on our match when we were young. That's common here, you know that now. Traditionally we don't choose our marriage partners, that's all decided on by our parents. I'd no reason to be any different and up until I met you, that arrangement was fine by me. It isn't a matter for questioning in our society. We simply accept it as the norm.'

'Then I met you and realised what falling in love and physical attraction meant. In our society one accepts arranged marriages and they do work and can become happy, lifelong relationships. Falling in love and choosing a partner here isn't a consideration. Love matches are few and far between and not a major concern when marriages are arranged. That must have become evident to you by now.

'I would have explained all this to you before we got married but you became pregnant before I'd decided to ask you to marry me. Would you have been happy to find out about Poppy and Kissie and your own pregnancy all at once? That was the question I was faced with when I returned after Papa's death. Would you have believed that I wanted to marry you for yourself then or would you think I was only marrying you to do the honourable thing by you? Think about it, darling. I didn't know how best to handle the situation.'

'Everything seemed to accelerate once we got involved. I hadn't the opportunity to take the relationship one step at a time. Sooner than I knew where I was, Papa died, I had to take over his duties here and then, to top it all, you became pregnant. Everything happened at once. I'd to come back here and face Mama and Kissie with the news that I'd got married and that wasn't a simple task. Please believe me, I haven't told you because I didn't want to, I simply did it because I didn't know how to tell you. The right opportunity never seemed to arise.'

'When you asked me at Christmas, I thought it would be better for you not to know when you were still carrying Milton. Truly, I'm sorry you've had to find out the way you have. Did Kissie tell you?'

'Yes, she did. But don't blame her though. She was just so sad and unhappy when she told me and I felt sorry for her.'

'Yes, I can see for you it's all a bit of a messy situation. Unfortunately what's done is done now and I'm asking you to try and not upset yourself about it. Please, my darling, tell me I'm forgiven?'

'I think I do understand, it's just a shock to me. You do love me, don't you?' Fiona sought that reassurance to keep her courage up.

'Of course I love you. You're my number one girl, aren't you?'

They locked themselves in a passionate embrace and Wil gently made love to Fiona. The long period of sexual deprivation leading up to Milton's birth and Fiona's subsequent recovery was at last past and they were once more intimate, passionate lovers. As long as they felt like that towards each other, nothing, not even Kissie, could break the magic they shared.

Chapter Ten

Sierra Leone's population was gripped in independence fever. As the all-important date grew nearer, the excitement heightened. Celebrations all over the country were being planned. The handing over of the British colony to the Sierra Leone People's Party, led by Milton Margai, was to take place on the twenty-seventh of April 1961. There would be an exodus of British government officers. Their posts would be taken over by newly appointed Sierra Leonean officials. Sierra Leone would be one of Africa's independent countries, run democratically by its own people.

In Kenema, parades would take place and functions were organised to mark this historic event. Fiona suspected little would change within the country, but the local people had high aspirations of what the new government would achieve once the colonial period ended.

Much of the country's wealth came from its diamond industry. In the previous ten years the Kenema and Sefadu areas had experienced a rush of people into those areas in search of diamonds. Locals were allowed to prospect under licence. In the 1950s it had been discovered that the alluvial deposits washed down in streams from the highland areas contained diamonds. They could be panned from the alluvium in the valleys in the Kenema and Sefadu regions.

Wil's tennis partner, Meynard, dealt in diamonds. Fiona had once asked him to show her some of the diamonds he had. How bitterly disappointed she had been when he opened up the safe and produced a cigarette tin and emptied some of the contents out for her inspection. She'd expected bright shining jewels to appear. Instead, they were a heap of small stones, like gravel. These, he explained, were industrial diamonds, not the gemstones she'd expected to see. To see some of the polished gemstones, she would have to go to the Diamond Corporation at Yengema or Tongo.

The Diamond Corporation ran a highly mechanised mining system and although simple, the yields were high. Local diggers were only licensed in the 1950s and this ended the government's monopoly. Up until then there had been widespread illicit diamond digging and smuggling but even though all diamonds should pass through government buying offices there was still much trade and smuggling in illicit diamonds. Back in 1956 the Alluvial Diamond Mining Scheme was set up to permit small-scale mining by indigenous people to operate in small groups of about four or five miners. The huge profits were worth the risk for poor people and farming was becoming neglected or abandoned in favour of chancing diamond digging. The country's soil was largely iron bearing, thus not very fertile which meant that most farming activities were marginal and consequently not very profitable.

The Sankolis were all invited to attend the independence celebrations being organised by the District Commissioner's office. Mama Nkozi said they must have new dresses made for the occasion and she would fly down to Freetown to purchase new stocks of material for the shop at the same time. She would spend the week there with Regina. It was then that Kissie suggested that the three of them have traditional dresses made the same. Fiona had reservations about this and said she'd make herself a new dress for the occasion if Mama Nkozi got her some nice material.

'I don't think I'd be comfortable in the local dress. I don't feel I'm entitled to wear it.'

'Don't be silly. It'll be fun, the family being dressed the same. It's quite in order for families to be dressed the same. Let's do it and surprise Wil.'

When Mama Nkozi returned from her shopping spree, she'd arranged to have new materials sent up by rail and when they arrived at the shop, Fiona went into Kenema to choose some lengths to make dresses for herself. Mama Nkozi had brought back lengths of fine satin material heavily embossed with gold patterns for the special Independence Day costumes. She'd purchased three lengths of material the same, but in different colours; green for herself, red for Kissie and blue for Fiona. The tailor made the costumes up for them.

On the eve of independence, they were invited to drinks prior to the lowering of the British flag ceremony and the raising of the new flag of Sierra Leone at midnight. This prestigious event heralded the start of the Independence Day celebrations.

Fiona went to don her new traditional outfit to match those of Mama Nkozi and Kissie. Wil took one look at it and said, 'Oh, no you're not wearing that!' He was cool and unruffled. Wil had a very placid nature and was soft spoken. Fiona knew he meant what he said.

'It was Kissie's idea. She thought it would be fun to be all dressed the same. She said it was quite usual for families to be dressed alike. Mama Nkozi bought the material specially when she was down in Freetown.'

'What Kissie forgot to tell you was that if I had more than one wife, then they would usually all dress the same. You'll likely see evidence of that tonight when some of the chiefs attend and also at the parade tomorrow. I don't want to turn up at the District Commissioner's party with what looks like three wives. Also, I don't really think you should consider wearing our national costume. How would you feel if I got all dressed up in a kilt? You would feel embarrassed I expect?'

'Yes, I suppose so. I didn't think you would be very keen, but Kissie wanted to surprise you and asked me to keep it a secret.'

'You just get dressed in one of your own frocks and I'll go and have a word with Kissie.'

Fiona realised that Wil was right in his objections. She should have never agreed to it in the first place. It was such beautiful material as well. Never mind, she'd soon manage to make some alterations to it to convert it into a short dress. She felt somehow humiliated by the episode and it took some of the excitement of the evening away. She wondered whether Kissie had planned the whole episode, realising that Wil would never have approved.

Kissie's reaction to whatever Wil said resounded through the house in a loud, angry voice. 'You're nothing but a spoilsport!' she screamed. 'You're all high and mighty now you've got a white wife. Your own people aren't good enough for you any more. I'm not going with you now to the party! What's the harm in her wearing our local dress?'

The shouting was followed by Kissie's bedroom door being violently slammed shut.

Fiona's stomach started to churn. Now Kissie was upset and there would be tension amongst the four of them. They'd all been looking forward to these celebrations. There had been such a build-up to this historic event and now the household was involved in petty quarrelling.

Wil came back into the bedroom. 'You heard the outcome I expect? Now she's upset and says she's not going.'

'Don't worry I'll go and see her and pour oil over troubled waters. She's basically jealous of me. I know what's really eating her. She won't ever be happy until she's ousted me. That's her ultimate goal.'

'Don't be silly. All this drama over a silly frock. Women are getting out of hand and I seem to be getting my share of it all,' Wil tartly replied.

Some smooth talking, coaxing and cajoling brought Kissie round eventually. Mama Nkozi intervened and spoke sharply and authoritatively to Kissie and that had the desired effect. She was obviously frightened of Mama Nkozi and wouldn't have answered her back.

'Let's all have a drink and I'll propose a toast to harmony in the new independent Sierra Leone and within the household as well. Won't you open a bottle of wine, Wil and we'll all feel better when we've sat and had a relaxing drink?'

So they all toasted in the new independent state before they set out for the official function. Fiona admired Mama Nkozi's and Kissie's green and red outfits. They both looked splendid in their costumes and matching headdresses. The flattery and the wine helped to bring Kissie round and Wil condescended to agree how beautiful the two of them were.

Harmony having been recaptured, they attended the function and cheered and celebrated the dawning of a new beginning for Sierra Leone. Independence Day was spent celebrating. There was a parade in the streets of Kenema and the District Commissioner and other dignitaries took the salute. All day the streets in Kenema were thronged with deliriously happy inebriated crowds. Later on they ate at a party which Meynard had organised. The party continued late into the night but as soon as darkness fell Wil took Fiona home with Milton as it was his bedtime. Wil returned to the party though where there was dancing and further rejoicing.

Storm clouds started gathering in the skies during May. The intense drought of the long dry season would shortly end. Some evenings when they were on the veranda, sheet lightning could be seen on the distant horizon accompanied by distant rumblings of thunder. Fiona was frightened of the thunder and lightning and was not looking forward to the storms. After several days of build up, the first storm of the season broke. It was preceded by a sudden wind blowing through the house and a deafening noise on the roof. They hastily closed all the windows and doors. Then forked lightning bolted from the skies to the ground in streaks of bright light, the like of which Fiona had only encountered once before; on her first night in Freetown. She was terrified and took to the bedroom, covering her head with the pillow. The thunder rolled heavily directly above her. The lights, which were dim at their best, dipped as each flash flared around them. The storm lasted about fifteen minutes and moved off abruptly. The heavy rain spewed off the roof onto the dry powdery soil. The noise woke Milton, but his cries could hardly be heard above the combined noise of rain pounding on the tin roof and thunder. He soon fell asleep again once the storm passed.

Wil took Fiona out onto the cool wet veranda and she could smell the freshness in the air from the settling effect the rain had on the dust-laden air, vegetation and trees. The thunder continued to drone on in the distance with some sheet lightning for another hour or so.

The frequency of the storms increased in June and July. With each passing storm Fiona's fear waned a little until she could eventually come to sit outside on the veranda and enjoy the spectacle. The brightness and intensity of some storms reminded her of firework displays. August saw the heaviest rainfall. Some days the moisture-laden clouds lay around the house and trees until the heat of the sun drew them high into the sky around midday. Some days it rained non-stop, but the precipitation was steady and didn't have the intensity of the tropical storms. The rains were warm, not like those from home. She enjoyed a stroll down the road whilst it rained, allowing the warm droplets to soak her. The heat and rain meant the humidity was at its highest.

The servants and their families nearly all succumbed to fevers and shivers and Fiona was left in charge of distributing malaria and headache tablets as necessary. The servants had warmed considerably to Fiona over the months. She was now able to understand most of their Pidgin English and could communicate reasonably well with them. They sensed that she was much less strict on them than the others and consequently they started to bring any troubles they had to her attention, seeking her to act as spokesman to 'the Master' (Wil) or 'the big Mama' (Mama Nkozi). She was also at home all day, whereas the others had limited time and interest to pursue the servants' problems. She felt genuinely sorry for them at times. They had so little and yet on the other hand she also envied them. They were happy and weren't subjected to the miseries of urban life and the Western rat race which civilisation seemed to inflict. None of the servants could read or write and they led such simple lives. Schooling wasn't compulsory. They learned their traditions and skills from the older members of their tribes and the secret societies when they were taken away for their initiation training and ceremonies. The garden 'boy', Jusu, had told her once that if only his children could go to school to be taught how to read and write, then he would be happy. Jusu was called the garden boy, but as gardens went, it was non-existent! He merely kept the compound around the house and kitchen neatly brushed and any encroaching vegetation at bay.

The 'small boy', Saffa, had approached Fiona about a bicycle. If only he could buy a bicycle, that would make him so happy! He could go to and from Kenema so quickly then. Of course he had no money and even if he could save some of his wages, it would take years to accomplish. By then, Fiona thought, he would be too old to ride it! Anyway she agreed to approach 'the Big Mama' on his behalf. He said he feared her too much to ask himself! This was obviously a major request when she broached the subject at dinner one evening. His aspirations were greater than his position merited. However, after some persuasion and assurance by Fiona that he was a diligent worker and he was keen and progressing well with his baking in the kitchen, plus he hadn't broken nearly so many dishes of late, Mama Nkozi agreed to speak to him about the financial implications.

Wil managed to buy a second-hand bicycle, a sturdy Rudge, from Meynard's son, Lamin. He said he didn't use it much and he would prefer to have the fifteen pounds cash rather than keep the bike. Saffa, who earned fifteen shillings a week, agreed that three shillings be docked weekly to pay for the bicycle.

The day that driver Lansana collected the bicycle and brought it home was one Fiona would never forget. Saffa's face literally shone he was so happy. Everybody on the compound joined in his delight and gathered round this prized possession to celebrate its arrival. Fiona hoped that the novelty would not wear off before he'd paid at least half of it! It was only when she asked to see him ride that she discovered he'd never been on a bicycle before and he couldn't ride it!

All the next week Saffa worked so well and he was so happy. No task was left undone and he went about his work eagerly. Usually the servants would go through periods when skipping chores was a regular habit so work had to be continually checked. Any spare moment he had he'd be out on the road practising. Fiona tried to show him how to ride it. Soon he could manage to be reasonably proficient to attempt going out along the Kenema road. Fiona warned him seriously about the dangers of passing vehicles and stressed that he must always keep to the left-hand side of the road for his own safety. He wobbled continuously, but managed to stay on.

About two weeks later Wil passed him on the road home and confirmed that he was indeed quite safe on the road. As soon as he saw Wil's approaching car he dismounted and carried the bicycle into the dense bushes at the side of the road! Kissie and Wil were still laughing about it when they reached home that evening.

It was now September and little Milton, Fiona's constant companion, was already seven months old. He was a robust, happy little child and was sitting up on his own and taking notice of all around him. His fat inquisitive little fingers were touching everything in reach and everything was transferred from his hand to his mouth. He'd two teeth already. The rains were slackening, but there were still the end of season thunderstorms. The roads were now tracks of slippery mud, deeply grooved by mammy lorry tyres. Travelling was even more hazardous than normal with a high probability of getting stuck, or slithering off the track into the bush. The workers, as Fiona still referred to Wil, Kissie and Mama Nkozi, had been using the Land Rover to and from work in Kenema and the Mercedes had been parked at the surgery since the onset of the main rains. They could use the car in and around Kenema because the main roads there were tarred but it was too dangerous to drive it on the mud roads because of the deep muddy potholes. The Land Rover had the advantage of four-wheel drive, if necessary, and had a much greater clearance, even though it was much less comfortable.

Thursday was Aruna's day for shopping and Lansana used to take him to Kenema every Thursday afternoon to replenish the groceries and bring them back. One particular Thursday in late September he received news that his brother had taken ill and he must return home. He immediately declined into a panic and wanted to leave but there was the shopping still to be done. He suggested that Saffa do it, but Fiona felt sure that wouldn't work out so she assured Aruna that if he told her what was needed, then she would go and then he would be free to leave. She couldn't ask him to give her a list because he wasn't literate.

So it happened that Fiona, hoisting Milton on her right hip, did the weekly shopping. Lansana knew all the stores to call at for the various items and the last stop was the Cold Store. While she was in the queue with Milton and Lansana, waiting to be served, a European lady came in and stood at the long wooden counter next to her.

'Hello, little fellow, what's your name?' she enquired of Milton.

'Oh, hello, this is Milton,' Fiona replied.

'You must be the doctor's wife, are you?'

'Yes, I am, how on earth do you know that?' Fiona replied, rather taken aback.

'Quite simple really. I know the doctor has a European wife and as there are so few European women in Kenema and I know most of them by sight, though not always to speak to, I put two and two together. I'm Judy Hughes by the way. It's nice to meet you!'

'I'm Fiona. It's nice to meet you as well. Do you live here in Kenema?'

'No, I live about thirteen miles out of Kenema on the Chrome Mines. It's out on the Hangha road.'

'You must be about ten miles from me then as we're about three miles out that road also, but not out as far as Hangha.'

Fiona's turn to be served came and while her shopping was being gathered together and packed into a large cardboard box, she chatted with Judy.

'Why don't you come and visit me one afternoon if you're not working? Do you have transport to take you?'

'I'd like that. Yes, I could easily arrange transport to fit in with the others. I don't see that as a problem at all. I'd really love to visit if you don't mind.'

'Good, then you can come and meet my little one.'

'Have you got a baby also?'

'A baby, yes, but not the human variety,' Judy laughed. 'I'm bringing up an orphaned chimpanzee and she's nine months old, but I call her my baby. She has to be looked after just like a human baby. She's very demanding and naughty though.'

'Oh, I'd love to see a baby chimpanzee,' Fiona eagerly replied.

'When would you like to come? Any time suits me. I only come down here about once a month, so I'm at home all the time.'

'I'm not sure when would be most convenient for our driver to take me, so it's difficult for me to give you a specific day right now.'

'Look, why don't you come up one afternoon next week? Doesn't matter to me which day it is. You take me as you find me. Just ask at the barrier and they'll give you directions to my bungalow. See you soon then?'

'Yes, thanks, see you next week.'

Lansana loaded up the box of groceries into the back of the Land Rover and off home they went. Fiona felt so happy to have met and spoken to Judy. She was the first British person she'd spoken to since she'd arrived in Sierra Leone. She was excited and looked forward to seeing her again. The shopping trip had been successful also and Fiona felt a sense of well-being when she'd packed away all the groceries with Saffa's help. He assured her he could cope adequately with the meals during Aruna's absence. They didn't know when he would return. It all depended on how ill his brother was. Fiona told Saffa that he must come and ask for her help if he got into difficulties in the kitchen or the work was too much for him.

That night when the others returned home Fiona was bubbling with her news. Usually she was waiting to hear from them what had transpired, if anything, during the day, but now for a change she'd got some news of her own.

'And she invited me to visit her next week sometime, depending on when you can spare me transport. She said I could go any afternoon. She's got a baby chimpanzee as well!' Fiona told them all excitedly.

'That's great for you.' Kissie sounded genuinely pleased. 'You haven't really made any friends since you've been here and you're tied to the house all the time. It'll be a nice change for you.'

'You can go any day you like, darling,' was Wil's response. 'We can come home in the car. The roads aren't very good yet but you take Lansana and the Land Rover and I'll drive us home, then it means you don't have to be back at any specific time. Did you remember to do the shopping in all the excitement?'

'Of course I did. In fact Lansana and I did very well and got everything Aruna wanted. How long do you think Aruna will be gone?'

'Hard to say, but I expect he'll be back Monday sometime.'

Wil was right, Aruna did return Monday mid-morning. His brother had died early Saturday morning.

Like so many of the natives, he'd died of tuberculosis, a disease which was still a major problem in Africa due mainly to malnutrition. Their poor staple diet of rice was a major contributing factor. The disease spread rapidly in families and communities. Wil explained to Fiona that the habit of spitting also spread this contagious disease. If only an awareness campaign to stop that could be initiated, then it would perhaps help. Fiona had at that time declared that although she found the habit of spitting deplorable, she considered that men openly urinating anywhere, as they did, was to her a much more disgusting habit. Wil had replied, 'Yes, to you it looks more serious and offensive, but it doesn't create the same health hazard as the spitting does!'

On Wednesday Fiona and Milton set off to visit Judy after lunch. Lansana drove them. The drive took about half an hour. They turned left off the main road at Mano Junction and carried through the small village of Bambawo where practically all the natives employed at the Chrome Mines lived. At the foot of the mountain range they arrived at the barrier which was the entrance to the mine property. The guard on duty gave Lansana directions on how to reach Judy's house. The house was high on the hillside and parts of the dirt road leading up to the house were exceedingly steep. They passed noisy machinery and an office block and eventually reached Judy's bungalow. She appeared immediately with a chimpanzee dressed in a nappy and rubber pants, running on all fours closely behind her, voicing loud grunts of disapproval at being left behind.

'Good, you managed to find me alright I see,' she said and at the same time bent down to pick up the chimpanzee and thrust her onto her hip, just the way Fiona was carrying Milton. 'This is my Jane.'

'No bother at all. But what a climb up to the bungalow from the bottom of the hill!'

'It's been very difficult in the rains for the vehicles to get up and down the hill. But once up here you see we have a beautiful view of the valley and beyond from the front of the house. Come through and look from the veranda.'

They entered the back of the bungalow through the kitchen and into the lounge area, then out onto the veranda. The view was indeed spectacular.

'You see those light brown patches down on the plain, they're diamond diggings I'm told and you're supposed to be able to see right to Liberia from here. All the bungalows here are set in this dense tropical forest which had to be cut down and cleared for the roads and houses.'

'Are there a lot of people here then?'

'No, not a lot, I'd say about twelve bungalows are occupied at the moment. There are quite a lot of empty ones and they are already overgrown.'

'Are there any other women?'

'Yes, at the moment there's six women and me and there's also five children of various ages.'

'Does that include or exclude Jane?' Fiona enquired.

Judy laughed out loud. 'Better watch what you're saying, my girl. I like to think of her as my baby, but that doesn't go down too well with some of the mothers. No, the five children are real children.'

Milton and Jane seemed quite fascinated by one another but Judy said that she couldn't really trust Jane completely with Milton.

'She's strong, you see and also she's got six teeth already and there's a chance she might just want to test them out and we wouldn't want that. It's best she's well supervised and not allowed too close to Milton. They're very like human babies and they develop about the same rate, but they are animals when all's said and done and she could take a tantrum and lose her temper and behave as an animal.'

'Let's go and make some tea, shall we? Or maybe you'd prefer something cold?'

'An electric kettle! Wow, that's quite a sight! You're really modern up here I see,' said Fiona with surprise. 'Have you got more electrical appliances?'

'Oh, we're pretty primitive up here on the whole, but we do have electric fridges, kettles, irons, toasters and wirelesses.'

'What luxury to have an electric iron as well.'

'I wouldn't quite call it luxury, but we get by. We've still got the wooden stove to cook on though. Haven't you got electricity then?'

'Yes, but only lights, and even then they're not all that powerful and often don't work.'

'Don't tell me you've got those awful irons that you put hot charcoal in?'

'I'm afraid so. I can't do any ironing at all because I'm terrified to use it.'

'But they're forever spilling out ashes and burning little holes in the clothes.'

'Don't I know that!' Fiona laughed. 'You know when I came here last year I'd absolutely no idea what I'd find. I wasn't prepared for any of this – I knew nothing about Africa really. You know, on my journey out here I wasn't even sure whether I'd be living in a mud hut or not.'

The two of them laughed and laughed there in Judy's kitchen as she made a pot of tea. Suddenly Fiona felt young and carefree, like her college days when she shared with the three girls.

'You know I don't think I've laughed so much since I came. I can't share a joke with them at home. They don't seem to understand what I'm laughing at or find funny.'

Although Judy was much older than Fiona, at a rough guess she'd have said forty-ish, she could capture her sense of fun.

'This really tastes like tea. I don't have tea at all at home. I'd a cup when I first arrived and it was awful. It's the condensed milk that makes it taste so bad. What kind of milk is this you've got? It's like real milk.'

'I use the powdered milk and make it up a pint at a time into a jug. I use either Dutch Baby or Klim and whisk it up with water and it's reasonably like pasteurised milk.'

'Where do you get it? We only use tinned evaporated or condensed milk. It's not too bad in coffee, but I can't take it in tea.'

'The Cold Store sells it and all of the Indian shops as well.'

'I must get Aruna, our cook, to get some when he goes shopping next and I can make some up and keep in the fridge for tea from now on.'

The afternoon passed quickly. They spent the time finding out about each other and Lansana had been entertained by Judy's small boy and had met other cooks and small boys employed by mine personnel.

'Won't you come over sometime and visit me?' Fiona asked when it was time to leave.

'It's not so easy for me because I'm stuck here without a vehicle, but if you don't mind, you just come up and see me. If you come again next week, we can take a walk down to the Club and you can meet some of the others. You don't have to say when. I'm always here and you can just arrive. How does that suit you?'

'Alright, that's very kind of you. I'll hope to come again next Wednesday, but don't worry if something prevents me. It's only if they need the Land Rover or Lansana that I wouldn't be able to come.'

'We've got a pool here as well at the Club, so bring your bathing suit.'

'I haven't got one.'

'Don't worry then. I'll ask around and we'll find somebody who's bound to have a spare one. Bring a towel in case we do and Milton can splash about in the baby pool. See you next week then with luck.'

The three workers were already at home when Fiona returned.

'How was it then?' they eagerly wanted to know.

Wil was outside to meet them when he heard the Land Rover approaching. 'Did you enjoy yourself and how did you find the monkey? It was quite disconcerting to come home and find no wife or son here to greet me.'

'Can we go again next week? Judy can't come here because she's got no vehicle, so she said I should visit her if that's possible.'

'I'm sure we can arrange that,' was Wil's reply.

'Milton enjoyed himself too. He was very interested in Jane the chimpanzee, but Judy was a bit scared she would be too rough and also she was worried she might just bite him, so we had to be careful. Milton's very tired now after such an exciting day out. I think I'll get him bathed and fed straight away and off to bed.'

As soon as they had dinner that evening several friends called round for drinks and a chat so it wasn't until bedtime that Fiona was able to tell Wil all she'd learned about Judy.

Chapter Eleven

Judy's husband, John, was with a British Geological Survey team who were mapping the country and they rented the accommodation from the Chrome Mine. John travelled around for one or two days at a time whilst she remained at the mine bungalow. Judy came from Cornwall and had a lovely South Country accent.

'You must have made a good pair then, what with your Scottish accent!' Wil declared. 'Has she got any family?'

'I don't think she has. She didn't mention any and I didn't ask. I'm sure if she had she'd have said so. You know she treats that chimpanzee exactly like a child. She even had nappies on it. That made me also wonder if she'd no family and she was maybe compensating in some way by treating the chimp like a child. It's quite sad, isn't it, if that's the case?'

'I wouldn't say that – you know how the British are fanatical about animals. Some of my patients in Nottingham were like that with dogs and cats. Maybe she's just one of them.'

'I hope so, but no doubt I'll eventually find out.'

'What's she planning to do with this chimp when it gets too big for her to keep?'

'Yes, she did tell me that she's due to go home around July next year when Jane will be about eighteen months old. She's already been in touch with some zoo in England and she's donating Jane to it. The zoo is going to arrange and pay for the flight and necessary documents.'

'Poor animal, destined for a zoo. It should be out in the hills free, don't you think?'

'Yes, I'm inclined to agree with you, but then when she got it, it was too small to fend for itself and the hunters had shot its mother. Sad, isn't it? She says that there are wild chimpanzees out in the forest around them, but she's not been able to see any, she can only hear them calling and shouting at each other. She reckons they're quite close as well sometimes. Do you think we've got chimps around here as well as the monkeys?'

'Of course they're around, but I expect they keep pretty well up into the forest for protection and also at a distance from the humans. So you obviously enjoyed your outing. It's certainly perked you up. You're more like you were when I first met you.'

'How do you mean? Do you think I've changed?'

'Mm, hmm, hmm,' he nodded. 'I think sometimes you seem a little sad and dejected looking. You've lost some of your sparkle.'

'Really?'

'Yes, maybe it's just what you need, some company around your own age?'

'Judy's quite a bit older than me. Maybe some of the other women will be younger than she is.'

'Maybe it's company of your own kind you need. Maybe you're getting a bit homesick, are you?'

'I don't think so. Perhaps I'm just getting older and more mature. Perhaps my husband doesn't pay enough attention to me any more. Perhaps I'm being taken for granted?'

'Come then, we'll soon sort that out,' he whispered as he drew her closer to him.

She immediately reacted passionately to his kissing and fondling and after an exhausting love making session Wil confided, 'If this is the reception I can expect after a visit to Judy, then maybe we should send you up there every afternoon!'

The next day Fiona pondered over what Wil had said. Was she really turning sad and dejected as he'd suggested? Since Milton's birth she'd devoted one hundred per cent of her time to him. She loved him dearly and he was such a joyous, happy little soul. He was contented and easy to look after. She'd never had to cope with nights on end of lost sleep, nor had he been a sickly, difficult boy. He'd no hang-ups about being tended by Mama Nkozi, Kissie, or any of the servants. Perhaps she would have been happier if they didn't have to share the house all the time with so many people. Friends and relations, however distant, were constantly coming and going. It was seldom that Regina's room was empty. In fact Wil had spoken only recently of the need for a couple of extra bedrooms. They needed one for Milton when he grew a bit bigger and also one for Poppy.

Apart from the constant coming and going of visitors, there were the long hours that Wil often had to work. He was so conscientious about his work that he often tried to cope with more than he was physically able to. Of course she knew before she arrived that he would be taking over his father's place, not only his work, but his household position. Family life amongst Africans was much tighter knit than the Western world was used to. With increased mobility and financial independence the 'civilised' world had seen a breakdown of the extended family unit and its importance. Families were less dependent on each other for support. The old fashioned family values and sharing were still fundamental to African culture. She realised she had to fit in with her new surroundings and their way of life. It was not feasible to expect to live alone with Wil and Milton as a complete family unit. Such an arrangement would be beyond the family's compre-hension. Perhaps if she could only have Wil to herself occasionally she'd be happier. Maybe she was selfish expecting to commandeer too much of his time. She had to admit to herself that she certainly did feel good after her afternoon with Judy. Maybe she had, unbeknown to herself, been slipping downhill a bit of late. Wil had noticed though.

The next week again saw Fiona and Milton set off to visit Judy. She'd looked forward eagerly to the trip. Judy said she'd been hoping that they would make it.

As promised, they had a walk to the Club in the afternoon. Judy had asked the other women to come and meet Fiona there. They were always keen to meet someone new so Fiona was introduced to the six wives living on the mine and their children. Initially they sat round the children's paddling pool so the smaller ones could splash about safely in the water. Milton was the youngest child there and the older children all wanted to play with him. He was in his element sitting at the side of the shallow pool watching the others play. One little Italian girl, Pasquelina, who was two, brought over plastic cups of water and they spent the afternoon pouring the water in and out of half a dozen brightly coloured containers. Fiona was the centre of attraction and all the women wanted to speak to her. She supposed that they probably knew all about each other so it was of more interest to them to find out about somebody else. The older children were able to swim and they were expending much energy playing around in the larger swimming pool with various rubber rings and a couple of inflated inner tubes.

The Club opened at three-thirty when the steward arrived for duty. Doreen, the underground manager's wife, explained to Fiona that the working day on the mine finished at three forty-five so the Club opened just in time for the men who wanted to come straight from work to have a beer. She said it was a popular time for most of the people to gather socially for an hour or so, then they could relax together, catch up on the day's events, if any, then walk home before dark for dinner. Doreen had brought a swimming costume for Fiona. It was a spare one and Fiona was very welcome to have it provided she wasn't offended! Judy had mentioned it to her over the weekend.

Just about four o'clock a Land Rover arrived at the Club and about eight men got out and sat around the tables which the steward had arranged outside on the Club's veranda. The women, children and Fiona also moved up to the veranda then. Doreen introduced her in turn to all the men present. There were other men also on the mine, some were still working on shifts and some others weren't regulars at the Club at this time. Judy, who had Jane with her, sat next to Fiona and tried to explain who was who, but with meeting so many new faces, it was difficult to fit everybody in place. Fiona felt that she could detect some slight distaste to Jane's presence at the Club. The children of course were all fascinated with her and they wanted Judy to let her down to play with them. In the end she relented, provided Noreen, the oldest, a little girl of eight, took charge.

'The trouble is if she gets over-excited, she might be too naughty with the smaller ones,' Judy said, 'but play where we can see and watch what's going on.'

Of course the children ignored, perhaps even forgot, what Judy said and in no time they had all disappeared round the side of the Clubhouse. Shortly the hilarity of the children could be heard as they were laughing and enjoying themselves. Then inevitably, one little boy, Mark, rounded the corner in tears. He ran up to Judy and sobbed, 'Jane's got my ball and she won't give it back to me.'

'Let's go and get it for you then!' Judy took his hand and away they went to retrieve the ball and restore harmony.

'Bloody monkey! Causes more trouble than all the kids put together.' Fiona overheard a male voice comment but she didn't know who'd passed the remark. She didn't yet recognise whose voice it was.

'It's such a shame,' Doreen turned to Fiona, 'that she treats that chimp just like a child. I feel sorry for her, you know, but I can understand and make allowances for her behaviour. She's up here alone most of the time when John's off working. Unfortunately some of the others here aren't very tolerant or understanding.'

'Hasn't she got any family then?' Fiona hastened to ask, now that the opportunity had arisen.

'No, they did have a baby I believe but she'd complications at the birth and they lost it and she was never able to have any more. They're such a nice couple as well. She must get quite lonely when he's out in the bush. The chimp is company for her and occupies a lot of her time.'

Judy returned with Jane then. Jane was obviously cross at having had the ball taken from her and was jumping up and down in protest. Fiona couldn't help thinking that the chimpanzee did in fact behave just like a spoilt child. They all wanted the same toy, simply because one of the others was playing with it. She'd seen such situations time and again causing rows and tears at school during her teaching practice.

The Italian lady, Fioretta, and her two children were first to leave. Fiona realised she spoke no English and had depended on her small son, Umberto, who was only five, to act as interpreter for her. Judy said that they seldom came to the Club on their own because Fioretta spoke no English and she was a very shy girl. Normally they only came when her husband could accompany them and he could then interpret to include her in the conversation.

Some of the men, particularly the bachelors, started to play darts; Judy and Fiona left to walk back up the hill to the bungalow. The Club was downhill from Judy's place so they had the steep climb back and Milton was now no lightweight on an uphill climb. Fiona could see that the narrow dirt road had been literally hewed out of the dense forest on either side of them. The soil on the roads was the same red-coloured laterite as they had at their compound. This forest was original, not secondary growth, and the giant trees, including palms and the less tall balsawood, various epiphytes and ferns crowded them in on both sides of the road.

'I'll make some tea before you go. It'll help to replace some of the moisture we've lost sweating up this hill. John's coming back tonight. He's only doing day trips out this week, but I don't suppose he'll be back before six. I was hoping he'd be able to meet you this time.'

'It'll be a shame to miss him, but I do want to get back before dark. I hope we'll meet soon though. Do you find it lonely when he's out so much? You're not frightened on your own, are you?'

'Not now. I'm used to it. Also it's better coming with him than remaining in Cornwall without him. I suppose I'd have to stay at home if we'd children, but we haven't, so I'm quite happy to be on my own some of the time here. Jane's a lot of company and she keeps me busy. Also there's the other women here who I see quite regularly at the Club. I've a night watchman who comes at night as well. I don't think he's really necessary, but John insists. I suppose knowing he's out there has its advantages, just in case I should take ill and needed to send him to one of the other houses for help.'

'You're not frightened of break-ins, are you? I believe European houses are good targets for petty theft.'

'Not here. The locals are so superstitious, you know. Many of them are frightened to come up the hill at night because they say the bad spirits live up here in the hills, so that reduces the threat of being broken into. I always try and let my small boy go before dark because he's frightened going down the hill at night in the dark. I kept him late one night and he'd to go home in the dark on his own and the next day he said that the spirits were after him on his way home and he was terrified. I tried to find out what he meant but all I could get out of him was that his head went all funny.'

'More likely he'd been helping himself to some of your spirits from a bottle to get that effect!' Fiona laughed. 'But having said that, I know from what Wil and Kissie tell me goes on at the surgery, they are very superstitious people and easily frightened.'

Judy made tea and they sat out on the veranda to drink it. There they got the benefit of a slight breeze blowing through the forest. Judy put Jane into a playpen in the living room and left her to her own devices while they sat out having tea. Milton sat down on the veranda floor beside Fiona.

'He'll soon be crawling about and then he'll get filthy from the floors. My clothes are never clean with Jane's hands and feet, especially with these red floors. Everything I've got gets plastered in this red Cardinal polish. Is that what you've got at home as well?'

'Yes, our floors are also all done in this red. I notice it on the soles of all our shoes in particular. We've got one or two of the Indian rush mats and they skid from under your feet if you're not careful with all the polish Kelly puts on our floors. They're fanatical about polishing the floors. I can see Milton's going to be covered in red when he's crawling around. The good news is I don't do the washing. I must say I lead a very idle life out here.'

'All us European women tend to. I think if we didn't have some kind of help we'd never cope. It's a far cry from home with all the modern electrical household goods we're used to having at our disposal. Also, you must think of it positively. You're supplying much needed employment and wages to someone. Are you happy living out here?'

'Yes, I suppose I am. You know I've not really asked myself that question. Everything's so new and different here and I suppose I'm still getting used to everything. It's all still a bit of an adventure for me.'

'How do you get on with always being with black people all the time? Do you fit in well with them? Do they accept you, or resent you? How do you cope with knowing that this is now your home?'

'You know, Judy, it's refreshing to meet somebody so forthright as you are. I suppose that's what I like about you. You're asking me all the questions everybody wants to, and nobody has the courage to. They pussyfoot around the fact that I'm married to a black person. They're maybe embarrassed.'

'Well, it's a touchy subject you must admit. I've never been known to be what you'd call discreet. John always says that I never know when's the time to keep my mouth shut!'

'You're actually the first white person I've spoken to since I came here last year. I'd have said I didn't miss the company of other white women but after last week's visit to you, I'm not sure that would be true.'

'What do you mean? Did I upset you?'

'No, that's just it. I was so happy when I got home after being able to gossip and chit-chat with you, that I realised that maybe I do miss the company. Even Wil noticed it and remarked on it. It's just that you understand when I'm joking. You're on my wavelength. Mama Nkozi and Kissie don't seem to understand what I mean if I joke. It's not that they're uneducated or anything like that. It's just that they're... well...'

'Different,' Judy butted in. 'Fiona, you've got to realise that you could say that about other nationalities in general. Look at the Italians who work here on the mine, you can't share a lot of jokes with them. They don't understand the subtleties of the British sense of humour. Take for instance the American sense of humour, we Brits don't always appreciate it and that's nothing to do with a language barrier.'

'I wish I could have been able to discuss such things with my mother before I came here. Mum wouldn't accept Wil at all.'

'What does she think now that you've been here for a year?'

'I don't know. I've never heard from her since I wrote and told her I was getting married. She doesn't even know about Milton.'

'Dear, dear, I'm so sorry to hear all this. Look, Fiona, can I give you a piece of good advice?'

'Yes, of course you can.'

'Don't mention your family rift to the other women here. It only gives them food for gossip and the less they know about it the better.'

'Do you think so?'

'Yes, I'm sure. There are some things that shouldn't be generally known like that and I certainly won't tell any of them.'

Suddenly there was much activity taking place in the trees above them. 'Oh, look, up in the trees there, there's a troupe of monkeys passing. You see them? They're leaping from tree to tree. They follow the same path, you know, when they travel past. They don't travel through the forest randomly, you know.'

The chatter of the monkeys high up in the branches alerted Jane and she started to jump up and down responding in her chimpanzee language. The monkeys seemed to call back, but also continued to pluck young leaves and shoots from the trees and eat them on their route through the forest trees.

'They are Colobus monkeys. They say they've never been able to keep one of them in captivity,' Judy told her.

Fiona stood outside and watched them. Milton was also interested. The Colobus monkeys were jet black with shaggy coats and long white tails. Around their black faces were frames of longish white fur. They were so agile as well, leaping from the top of one of the tallest trees and landing with great precision into the branches below. How gracefully they managed to perform these circus-style acts. The troupe eventually all passed into the forest beyond.

'There are red Colobus monkeys as well and they are chestnut-red coloured where these you've just seen are white. Jane loves it when the monkeys are around. I expect it reminds her of her background.'

'We must get going now,' Fiona exclaimed when she realised it was already half past five. I like to get Milton in bed around half past six. He'll be tired tonight with all the activity. He was last week also.'

'You'll come next week, won't you?'

'Yes, I'd love to if you don't mind having me?'

'I enjoy the company. It's something to look forward to and you've no problem getting here, have you? I hope John arrives soon as we're going down to have dinner with Marie and Ron tonight. That's the Irish woman who was at the pool this afternoon with the three little girls. I've made Cornish pasties to take down there for them tonight. It's easier for us to go to them than have them all up here, then it doesn't interfere with the girls' bed times. Poor Marie, she's struggling terribly with lessons for the girls. I think it's a bit beyond her to tell you the truth, but she didn't want the family split up and the girls going to boarding school so young.'

'That's interesting. I'm a teacher. Maybe I can give her a bit of help if she's really struggling?'

'You'll be a gem of a find for Marie. I'm sure, if you offer any help. I'll mention it to her tonight and see what she says.'

'You do that and I'll see you next week again.'

They got back home just after six. They passed a Land Rover on the way down the hill and Fiona realised that it must be John on his way home to Judy. At least Judy would have him back on time that night.

Mama Nkozi was home and busy with a couple of friends, chatting and having drinks in the lounge when Fiona and Milton arrived back. She said that Wil and Kissie would be much later. They were round at Meynard's playing tennis and would be staying there for dinner.

Fiona felt a little deflated by that. She was quite excited and wanted to share the afternoon's events with Wil. As it happened, she had gone to bed before they eventually returned.

The events which took place the following week when she went to visit Judy took Fiona completely by surprise. Her arrival was eagerly awaited. Judy explained that she'd brought up the subject with Marie about Fiona being a teacher and that she'd offered assistance. Marie was certainly interested to hear that and would be grateful for any help. Ron, Marie's husband, had mentioned this to the manager of the mine and he had suggested that the company would pay for Fiona's services if she was interested in coming to teach the children on a regular basis. During the course of the week, the staff concerned had been consulted and if Fiona liked then they could offer her a position teaching the school-age children on the mine compound each weekday morning. They would even supply transport to take her there daily. They could simply reorganise their twice-daily mail run to Hangha to accommodate her teaching times.

Fiona was stunned, yet overjoyed. Judy took her down to the mine office to meet the manager, who put the proposal to her. She eagerly accepted and confirmed she'd love to help out. There would be five children altogether – Marie's three little girls and two boys. The two boys, both aged five, were not getting any schooling at all. The class of five would consist of three five year olds, one six year old and one eight year old. What a dream size of class that would be after coping with classes of between thirty and forty in Nottingham. So it was that she started to teach her little class of five students at the Chrome Mine.

Wil welcomed the opportunity that gave her something constructive and interesting to occupy her time. Marie had offered to look after Milton during her teaching hours, but they decided that he should remain at home with the boys in the morning. They asked Aruna if his wife would help out and he was delighted. His elderly wife, Fatima, was about forty and all her children were now grown up and she was used to looking after several of her grandchildren. The money she earned was also very much appreciated.

Marie had been teaching her three girls through a correspondence course run by an educational establishment in Britain specifically for Britons abroad. The curricula and textbooks were already set out so Fiona took over where Marie had reached. With her experience she was able to include extra-curricula activities to expand on the basics set out. The Clubhouse was designated the schoolroom from nine o'clock to one o'clock daily since it only opened as the Club from three-thirty.

By December, Fiona and the school had become an accepted part of life at the Chrome Mine and the three mothers were happy for the children to be learning and progressing so well. Little Umberto, the five-year-old Italian boy, was improving with his English also.

Chapter Twelve

The excitement of Christmas was building up. This was little Milton's very first Christmas and Fiona's second away from home. Funny, she still thought of Scotland as 'home'. They made decorations for the Club during class as well as Christmas cards, all of which added to the excitement. Letters were composed and posted to Santa Claus in the North Pole. She loved to watch the children's faces as their enthusiasm for the preparations for Christmas advanced. They had an air of honest simplicity and innocence. Noreen, at eight, knew that Santa Claus wasn't real, but even so, she concealed the secret from the little ones. It was a secret she shared with Miss Fiona, as the children called her. They cut and adorned a tree branch with little decorations they made and this served as their Christmas tree. They made the little schoolroom very festive.

The arrangement for leaving Milton at home with Fatima was working well and all in all, life in the Sankoli compound was happy and harmonious. They, too, were looking forward to Christmas and the arrival of Regina, Brima and the children from Freetown. Poppy had been home at times throughout the year and Fiona had become quite attached to her so she was looking forward to this Christmas time. Regina was eager to see baby Milton. Fiona had hoped to pay a visit to Freetown during the year and take Milton down but somehow that had never materialised. Of course, Milton wasn't so little any more. He was now a sturdy ten-month-old and keen to be on the move all the time. He was getting frustrated by his own inability to get about fast enough under his own steam. His crawling attempts were too slow, but he persevered. He was anxious to be more mobile but his legs weren't quite ready to take off on their own. As Judy had predicted, his legs and hands seemed permanently red from the floor polish. Added to that his dirty little hands wanted to interfere with and examine everything. He had eight teeth and they were used to test everything he could lay his hands on. Fortunately there were no ornaments around to be broken. She thought about the havoc those small interfering hands could wreak if they ever got loose in her mother's house with all her china and ornamental knick-knacks strategically placed within grabbing distance of a small child.

'I wonder if I'll hear from Mum this Christmas?' she asked Wil in bed one night.

'I very much doubt it. Did you send her a card again this year?'

'Yes, I did. At least it's an attempt on my side. She could just send a card.'

'I think you're hoping for a bit too much after all this time.'

'I wonder how they all are?'

'Just the same, I expect. Things and people don't change all that much in a couple of years, you know.'

'No, I suppose not.'

The mine had organised their Christmas dinner for Sunday the twenty-fourth. It was an evening affair to be held on the grounds outside the manager's house. It was to be a traditional English Christmas dinner and all the women were co-ordinating the event. Judy had volunteered to make mince pies. The Sankolis were invited also, but Mama Nkozi and Kissie said they wouldn't go because relations would be calling then and also Regina and Brima would be at home.

School closed on the Friday before Christmas for two weeks over the festive season. The family arrived up from Freetown on the Thursday and from then on the house was a chaotic hub of activity and celebrations. Milton had two small nursemaids in Priscilla and Poppy who both wanted to mother him. Little Lahai, now four years old, was getting too big and independent to be nursed. Lahai would also play with Milton but their games usually ended in tantrums, both wanting possession of the same toy. In spite of that, the four children played well together. Old Fatima was relieved of her duties for those two weeks now that Fiona was on holiday.

Daily, they either entertained callers and relations or they themselves would be calling on friends locally. They all made the Christmas trip on Boxing Day up country as they had done the previous year. At least Fiona was better prepared this time for the inadequacies of the bush toilet facilities.

On Christmas Eve Wil and Fiona attended the mine's Christmas dinner. This proved to be a truly British Christmas party with turkey, flaming Christmas pudding and mince pies. Drinks and snacks, carefully prepared by the ladies, were served on arrival. This was Wil's introduction to the mine personnel. There were some of the European staff there that Fiona hadn't met, particularly the bachelors and men whose wives were not accompanying them on their tour of duty. Fiona knew all the women.

The Christmas dinner celebrations that night included only the European staff. None of the Sierra Leonean employees were there. There was very little social contact with the local employees out of working hours. This was because the managerial staff in charge of all aspects of the mine workings were hired on contract from the London office. Local employees were nearly all unskilled labourers and neither spoke, nor understood much English.

That night the usual situation was reversed; Wil was the only black in an all-white group. Usually it was the other way round for Fiona where she was the outsider. Wil was strategically placed next to the manager at the dinner table. Judy said that was probably planned so that none of the staff would grasp the opportunity from the informality of the occasion to vent some personal gripe, particularly when tongues might be well-oiled with free liquor! At midnight they toasted the arrival of Christmas Day and threw streamers around. Wil had enjoyed himself and found the crowd to be pleasant and interesting. The manager had even offered to give him an underground tour if he had the time and inclination. He'd given Wil a general overview of the mine and its history.

Production had been declining due to the low chromite prices on world markets. All the material they extracted was railed to Freetown where it was shipped out. The chromite was extracted from underground. Originally they had been able to work opencast, but now all the material came from the underground workings. The material was sorted manually on conveyor belts and crushed in the crushing mill before being railed.

The company had a high standard of social responsibility towards its local employees. Most of them were housed in company-built accommodation in Bambawo, the small village at the foot of the Kambui hills. They provided food rations weekly to each employee. This was usually a rice ration with either dried fish or tinned pilchards. They also held a medical clinic every fortnight and one of the missionary doctors from Segbwema Mission Hospital was in attendance. The ex-pat staff attended the Mission Hospital if they were in need of medical care.

He asked Wil if his surgery queues were also like the ones he'd seen at the Mission Hospital and the fortnightly clinic. Wil confirmed that he also met long queues of sick daily, but that many still only trusted the healing powers of the traditional witch doctors.

The party was still in full swing when they left after one o'clock. Some were beginning to be the worse for drink by then, but it was obvious they intended to stretch the celebrations out as long as possible. They were those who didn't have to rise at dawn with boisterous children!

The new year saw the Sankoli household settling down once again to the usual routine. The house quietened down considerably with the departure of the children to Freetown. Poppy had stayed on an extra two weeks though and was of considerable help to Fatima with Milton.

Progress at school for Fiona was steady and rewarding. Her five little students had great respect for her and clearly enjoyed their lesson. On Wednesdays, she continued to see Judy. They had now become firm friends and Fiona treated her as mentor and confidante. What Fiona valued most about their relationship was Judy's forthright and honest opinions. Judy was twenty years older than Fiona, but she handled the relationship they had on an equal basis and didn't succumb to treating her as an inexperienced minor, as her parents had done.

After class on Wednesdays, Judy would walk down to the Club with Jane and bring sandwiches for their lunch. Later on some of the women and children would come to the pool to swim and chat. Fiona picked up many sewing tips during these sessions and was able to borrow dress patterns which improved her sewing attempts. She had become quite adept on the old machine at home and now made all her own clothes and quite a few for Milton.

Fiona found that most of her time was now occupied. Very different from the previous year when she'd no Milton, no job, no sewing and no real friends. The mine had a small library section which was a source of reading material when she had time. The women also passed on any British magazines which relations sent them. Although they were a bit old, she liked to page through them to see what fashions and information they contained. She also enjoyed reminiscing with the women about what commodities they missed. Sylvia said she missed fresh vegetables and apples; Marie missed chocolate and sweets; Judy missed 'real' shops and department stores which sold clothes. They complained together about the discomforts of their primitive way of life – no one complained about missing the cold, wet British weather though!

Milton took to his feet just after his first birthday. He didn't seem to miss Fiona when she was out at work. There were always so many people around and he'd never been a clinging child. He'd always let any of the family or servants look after him.

There was a constant coming and going of staff at the mine. Someone was always either going home on leave or returning for another tour of duty. Fiona got caught up in the excitement, particularly when it was one of the women due to go. Her three little girls, Bernadette, Kerry and Noreen, went in March with their parents to Liverpool and Dublin, but were almost immediately replaced with two little boys of six and seven who had just arrived. Reuben was seven and his mother had intended to remain in England with him so he could attend school, but with Fiona now on hand and giving lessons, the whole family could come out. So for a time her class was all boys.

When any of the women returned from England, Fiona loved to hear their first-hand accounts of home. Soon it would be Judy's turn to go and Fiona knew she would miss her most. She felt a sadness for Judy because tinged with the eagerness to return home was the impending sorrow she would experience when giving Jane up to the zoo.

It was about three weeks before Judy was due to leave that the Club organised a curry lunch. It was in part a farewell for Judy and John, coupled with a welcome back for Marie and Ron Gallager and the girls. The Sankolis were all invited to the lunch, but it coincided with an invitation they had received from a relation in Bo. Somehow, it came about that Fiona would attend the mine lunch and the others would go to Bo. Fiona couldn't quite determine whether it came about of her preference to spend the afternoon with the Europeans or whether it was that Wil preferred her not to accompany them. There was no animosity over the arrangement. Wil said he would like to take Milton because they were visiting relations who would be disappointed if the child didn't accompany them. Judy suggested that Fiona stay overnight and accompany them that Sunday evening to a film show at the Diamond Corporation mine at Tongo. John seemingly had a standing invitation to attend when they ran a film on occasional Sundays for their own staff. This arrangement was agreed on and Fiona set off that Sunday quite looking forward to her day's outing. She was keen to see Marie and the girls again and to find out how their three months' holiday had passed. She was eager also to find out if Marie had in fact been in every shop in Liverpool and Dublin as she'd threatened to do before leaving the mine back in March. She'd told Fiona she would shop, shop and shop for the entire three months to make up for the year spent in Bambawo.

Mama Nkozi, Kissie, Wil and Milton had set off early that morning and Fiona happily waved them all off. She was glad that Wil hadn't raised any objections to her going to the curry lunch at the Club instead of accompanying him. She knew the conversation would undoubtedly revolve round sickness and medicines and patients past and present – a conversation which she couldn't really participate in. Politics would be another of the main topics of discussion. They would no doubt have long discussions on how the country was coming along under its own new rule and the concern over the health of the ageing Prime Minister, Sir Milton Margai, and also the increasing support that Siaka Stevens, leader of the opposition All People's Party was raising.

Like the Christmas dinner, the curry lunch was attended by all the staff. An array of side dishes to accompany the chicken curry covered a whole table. There were dishes of chopped tomato, onion, red and green peppers, orange, banana, mango, pawpaw, avocado, peanuts, coconut and chutney. It was difficult to fit all these side dishes on to one's plate. The curry was hot and needed the help of the side dishes to cool it down!

After lunch she joined in some ball games in the pool with the children and a few of the adults. Some were playing darts and the rest just sat around chatting and drinking beer. Marie said in some respects she was glad to be back again after three months of living with and visiting both her and Ron's relations.

'It wasn't so bad when we stayed with my parents outside Dublin because the girls could run about in the countryside, but when we were at Ron's parents in Liverpool,' she'd confided to Fiona, 'they're under our feet all the time. Mind, it's very good of them to have us all staying with them because having five extra in the house puts them out considerably and upsets their normally quiet life. It'll be good just to be on our own again rather than with people all the time and get settled back into some routine.

Where's Milton today? He must be growing big and walking by now, is he?'

'Oh, yes, he's into everything. He started walking just after you went home. Wil's taken him today to Bo. They've all gone to visit some relative there who's involved in some kind of medical administration. The conversation there will revolve round medicine and politics I expect. I'm going to stay overnight with Judy and am going up to Tongo tonight to the film. I've never been before. Just think, it'll be my first film show in years. Are you going or not?'

'No, we won't be going. We're still getting over the travelling and sorting out things at the house. I'll be glad to see the girls off my hands in the morning as well. Thank goodness you've taken over the lessons now, I don't think I could cope any more with them. I think I'd have had to stay at home with them and put them to school now if you weren't doing it. Are there others going tonight, do you know?'

'I believe the mine is laying on transport for some who are going, but I don't know who. Apart from living with relations, how was your leave in general? Was the weather reasonable?'

'I really enjoyed it. We didn't get particularly good weather. Quite a lot of rain and it was cold, but that didn't stop us getting out and about. The shops were such a treat! Being able to go and buy things you want is such a luxury after being here for a year. You start to appreciate a lot of things they take for granted at home. Like going to the tap and drinking the water, and having running hot water. Then there's TV, we could use a TV here! It would be nice to sit down in the evenings and watch TV.'

'Would you like to stay at home now?'

'Yes, I would, but then Ron wouldn't earn as much as he does here. We're saving up for a deposit on a house. Maybe at the end of this tour, if we don't squander all our money on booze at the Club, we might have enough saved up. That's the main reason we're out here, to save the extra money we make. The theory is we can save while we are out here because there's nothing to spend it on, but Ron smokes and drinks twice as much as he does at home, so it's a catch-22 situation.'

In all, there were six from the mine who went to the Diamond Corporation Club for the film that night. Fortunately, no long drinking session followed, and as soon as the film ended at nine-thirty they all returned home. Next morning John was up and off for seven and left Judy and Fiona having their morning tea on the veranda which looked down on the plains in the distance. The view was spectacular. Dense white cloud lay on the plains below and the only visible land was green hillocks protruding through the cloud cover making them look like little islands surrounded by white sea. The bright orange sun was slowly climbing higher in the sky and as its heat intensified, so the white misty clouds dissipated, revealing eventually the fresh green plains of the valley in the distance below them.

'Not long to go now and you're off. I'm going to miss you when you go. I'm not looking forward to it. I suppose that's selfish of me, but I do hope you enjoy your holiday.'

'Two weeks today we travel down to Freetown. We'll get Jane off first and then have a few days there before we fly home.'

'Will you go and see her in the zoo when you go home?'

'Definitely, as soon as we can.'

'When do you expect to be back again?'

'John's still got quite a bit of surveying to complete up country, but we could be back around October. We've timed it nicely to miss the worst of the rainy season, and we should get some of the good weather at home.'

'Will you be in Cornwall all the time?'

'Yes, apart from trips to the zoo and perhaps a few days in London, we'll be at home in St Ives. I expect the cottage will need a good clean out after the summer visitors. Our next-door neighbour has the key and lets it out to summer visitors as she likes. It brings in enough income to pay the rates while we're away. When do you think you'll go home for a holiday?'

'Goodness knows. I'd not even thought about it until I started to work here and there's always somebody getting ready to go. It's only since then I've wondered when I'll ever go back. I haven't anything to go back for now that there's this family rift. Mum obviously hasn't come round and I can't ever just turn up with Wil and Milton.' Fiona laughed a little trying to visualise the comical side of the seriousness of her situation and make light of it.

'But when you're older,' said Judy thoughtfully, 'you're going to want to see that rift healed surely? Your parents must still be quite young, aren't they? Have you ever considered how you might feel if one of them were to die and you'd not righted things between you? I know it's a bit extreme to say this to you, and I hope it will never come to that, but maybe you should be careful not to let this run out of hand for too long.'

'Look, Judy,' replied Fiona, 'I've thought about it all often and I really don't know how best to handle it. You see it's easiest just to leave things as they are. At least it's not causing any more animosity by ignoring it. Goodness,' she suddenly exclaimed, 'have you seen the time? I'd better be off to school. Thanks for a lovely weekend! I'll see you Wednesday as usual?'

'Yes, of course.'

Chapter Thirteen

Suddenly the front door opened and Isobel and Stanley were home. Fiona stopped reminiscing immediately. Those vivid memories of such a painful time went. It was like quickly closing shut a book she had opened and had been paging through. There she was again, back in the familiar surroundings of Isobel's house. Fiona was in control of her emotions again by then.

'Gosh is it that time already? How was the pictures? I'll go and put the kettle on for tea. Mum's been round with cake and shortbread.'

'It was a cowboy and I find them a bit boring. They're all the same and the place was packed. We were so far down that we just about got covered in the dust from the horses' hooves as they went past on the screen. How was Ian? Any trouble?'

'No bother at all. Bruce got him all excited just as he was going to bed, but then that's nothing new.'

Isobel opened the tin that Mum had left on the kitchen table. 'Oh good, some fruit cake. Do you want some?'

'No thanks, I'll get it at home. You keep that for yourselves.'

After tea they sat and chatted then Fiona said, 'I'd better be off home now.'

'Hang on and I'll walk down the road with you. It's time I was off as well. I'll see you down at the boat in the morning sometime,' Bruce said to Stanley as he put on his jacket.

'Look, Fee,' he said as they walked down the street together, 'let's go out a drive tomorrow afternoon and try and sort this out.'

'Fine, what time?'

'I'm going down to the *Endeavour* in the morning to do some jobs, then I'll come round after lunch, latest three. We can take a drive out on the road a bit if it's a fine day and maybe have a bit of a walk as well. Think about what I said to you tonight though. I really meant it when I said I want to marry you.'

That night Fiona lay awake carefully thinking over the events of the evening. Deep down she knew how comfortable she'd become with Bruce. He'd been around for so long and he'd been her 'partner' so to speak over the last few years. He was a good chap and dependable and she had known for some time now that he'd been edging towards the question of a more serious relationship between them. She'd been careful to keep him at arm's length. She never wanted to experience again all the heartache that she'd gone through with her marriage to Wil. She was safe the way she was leading her life – she had her job and she lived with her parents. She did love Bruce without doubt, but he didn't fire up inside her the kind of passion and blind desire she'd felt for Wil when they had first been lovers. Look where that blinding love had led! Maybe that kind of passion was only for the young and reckless, a physical magnetism which once it had, like some raging fire, burned itself out, left nothing. Perhaps that was what Wil and her had experienced together. A physical sexual force so strong it overtook them like an addictive drug and they'd both succumbed to its power, needing more and more of each other. Once that fever had subsided they were left with nothing else in common to keep them bonded together. Perhaps if she had never fallen pregnant, then time would have proved to them their marriage wasn't viable. Yet, through all that unhappiness she felt she'd gained strength, maturity and understanding out of it. Her grief for little Milton was always a part of her, locked into her heart and memories. Tonight had brought all the past back to her so vividly.

She'd been at home nearly six years now and led a comfortable, carefree, relatively full life. Work had been her saviour. She'd always enjoyed teaching and she'd given all her energy to that and was now well respected at school. She'd deliberately closed her mind to relationships and complications that could involve her emotions. She lived within the constraints of routine. The predictability of that routine sheltered her from emotional exposure. Relationships and involvement were the same as hurt and heartache to her. Bruce had slowly crept in over the years, but he'd never pushed himself forward, almost as if he was waiting for the right time to make a positive move to secure her love. Would she be able to provide him with the happiness he deserved? Could she free herself completely from her past? Did she really deserve this second chance? They had so much in common and their backgrounds were the same and she knew that both families would approve. She knew she couldn't deceive him over her African past. Mum had chosen to deny its existence but she had to be honest with Bruce. He may no longer want to accept her once he knew her secret past.

She already felt some relief at having started to unburden herself to Bruce. Even though she'd succeeded in pushing it into the back of her mind over the last six years, the benefit of sharing all her pent-up grief and shame was therapeutic. She'd never talked about Milton to anyone since leaving Sierra Leone but the unremitting grief she felt remained even though it was unexpressed. Deep down she'd blamed herself and nurtured unjustified hostility to the thought of entering any form of male relationships. Maturity had helped her to recognise and accept her shortcomings. She still felt guilty that her marriage had failed. Initially she'd blamed Wil, without adequate cause, but eventually she blamed herself for not making sufficient effort. Perhaps she found it difficult to accept any failure on her part. Trying to achieve perfection in her life and setting herself such high standards had blinded her to the fact that she wasn't the cause of what had happened. Her desire to be in control meant her self-criticism was harsh. She'd felt guilt which stifled her ability to release herself from the shame of the failed marriage.

'Were you late last night?' Mum asked her when she got up.

'Yes, it was after midnight. Isobel says thanks for the baking. She'll bring the tins back at the beginning of the week. How was your whist?'

'Just the usual crowd, but it was good. Are you doing anything special today?'

'I'll go down the street and get what shopping you want, or do you want to come as well? Later on Bruce will be round. He wants to go out a drive if it's not raining.'

'Yes, I'll walk down town with you. I don't need much today.'

Later on, around two-thirty Bruce came round and after chatting to Archie for at least half an hour, they set off along the road in the Elgin direction. He drove into the suburbs of the town and then turned into Cooper Park.

'Let's walk round the park, it's a nice afternoon and quite warm. Do you fancy going on the boats on the pond?'

'Not really. Don't you get enough of boats and water during the week? What about going along the river bank rather and leave the car parked here?'

'Fine.'

She took the arm he offered and they crossed out of the park and along the narrow footpath which led towards the riverbank. The trees on the opposite side of the river were covered in different shades of green leaves and the gardens of the houses leading down to the water's edge looked particularly colourful with early summer flowers. The grass was growing wild on both sides of the path. They strolled slowly along behind the football grounds. The Saturday match was in progress as they could hear the noise of the enthusiastic supporters cheering on their teams. They crossed the river further down over the footbridge and spent some time gazing down into the flowing waters below. Once across the river they reached a wooden bench which they sat on.

'Do you want to finish your story now we're alone again? It's nice and peaceful here.' He put his arm round her shoulder and turned to face her.

Chapter Fourteen

That Monday afternoon after the curry lunch she got home as usual about one-thirty, before Wil, Kissie and Mama Nkozi had left the house after their lunch to return to work. Milton was pleased to see her, but Fiona noticed he hadn't been unduly disturbed by her night's absence. They had spent an enjoyable day at Bo and had only got back home around eight-thirty. Milton had fallen asleep in the car and Kissie had put him straight to bed.

Some family crisis had called Kelly away and he wasn't expected back until the next day. The upshot of that meant the washing hadn't been done, which wasn't exactly a major disaster. It could wait until the next day. Aruna always kept Fiona's lunch warm for when she returned at one-thirty because the others ate at one. As soon as she'd eaten she saw them return to Kenema for the afternoon, then she thought she'd clear up the dirty dishes and take them out to the kitchen for Saffa to wash. Because Kelly wasn't there she checked to see if everything else was in order and if there was anything needed urgent attention. She collected all the dirty clothes into a large zinc bath which she left in the kitchen for Kelly to do when he returned the next day.

She went to make up Kissie's bed to make the rooms tidy. That's when it hit her. She stopped dead. She ran back into her bedroom and there, sure enough, the bed was all nicely made up, but Milton's cot wasn't. Mama Nkozi's bed wasn't made up either. She suddenly felt too sick to think properly. Wil certainly wouldn't have made his bed when he got up, that was certain. Wil hadn't slept in his bed last night. That only left one explanation.

Fiona was stunned. The only person who could confirm this was dear little Milton and he, conveniently for Wil and Kissie, couldn't speak and wouldn't understand.

She made the beds up hastily, glad that the servants wouldn't find out what had happened. How unlucky for Wil that Kelly should be away today of all days! Wil must have thought she'd never find out she realised bitterly as she held back tears of rage and disbelief. My only night away from home and see how he behaves, she thought. She busied herself in the house, working at a speed which only ended up in bringing her out in a hot sticky sweat. She felt she needed the manual activity to work off some of her pent-up anger.

Eventually she sat down and tried to think hard. Milton would no longer sit on her knee for any length of time, he needed a bit of action. The only time he was still nowadays was when he was asleep. She mixed herself a glass of orange squash and went out to her favourite chair on the veranda. What should I do now? she muttered to herself. Her mind raced and became so active she ended up having an imaginary conversation between herself and Wil, speaking for herself and answering herself back for him. So intense were her thoughts that she became aware of actually conversing out loud, instead of in her mind. In the end she just sat and sobbed. All of a sudden she felt so lonely. The gay mood of the weekend turned to despair. All her thoughts turned negative and she felt genuinely betrayed. When her tears dried up she felt limp and devoid of any energy and emotion. How do I tackle this? she wearily asked of herself. If he denies it, he's a liar, and if he admits it, where do we go from here? The only time she was able to get him on his own was in bed. Other times he's flanked by his mother and Kissie. A scene out of the confines of the bedroom would involve all four of them and in the end she expected the odds against her to be three to one. The other two would surely side with him.

Fiona began to consider the implications of the relationship. Whatever transpired, Kissie would always be there as part of the family. She was firmly entrenched and invaluable for Wil's surgery. The only way Fiona could see of getting 'rid' of her was for her to find a husband, but that seemed remote. There didn't seem anybody around. Kissie was obviously quite content to play a waiting game, hoping eventually to oust her. On the other hand, Wil and Kissie might be quite happy to have a three-way relationship. This was quite acceptable in Sierra Leone. How belittling it would be to become one of two wives, practically part of a harem! She came to the decision that she didn't know how to handle the situation properly, if there was in fact a 'proper' way to deal with such an event. Maybe best ignore it? Eventually she decided to do nothing until she'd thought things out better.

That Monday evening came and went as normally as possible. Fiona might have been accused of being slightly subdued, but with the evening's discussions revolving round the trip to Bo and the curry lunch, it wasn't too difficult to keep the evening on a pleasant level.

She could hardly think about anything else all day Tuesday. On Wednesday at one, when class finished, she started off up the hill towards Judy's bungalow.

'Come up the road to meet us?' Then Judy noticed she was crying. 'Whatever's the matter, Fiona? What's wrong?'

'Can we go to your house instead of staying at the Club today? I don't feel up to facing any of the others today.'

As they walked back up towards Judy's she blurted out her story.

'What do you think I should do? Do you think I should tackle them? I just don't know what to do for the best.'

'Let me make tea first and I'll think about it.'

Fiona settled down and Judy sat next to her. 'I think you've done well up to now not to explode in front of him, but that would only make matters worse I expect. She lives with you all as part of the family and she works with him all day and those are two things which, whatever happens, aren't going to alter. She's been very cunning and it seems to me she intends not to let go of him at any cost. You can stop the affair going on at home, but they're at work all day together. It's a messy situation. The trouble is, my girl, you've married into a completely different culture. There's this huge gap between your two cultures. The initial powerful attraction you had for each other bridged that cultural gap. Whatever you do don't take offence at what I'm going to say to you. I'm too fond of you to jeopardise our friendship and I don't want to add to your hurt, but if you really want my advise, then I have to speak plainly and painfully to you. Africans and Europeans are different. It's not a case of superiority or inferiority or different colours, but I mean there are fundamental differences. Their culture and our culture aren't the same. Their values, way of life and traditions mean they can accept certain behavioural patterns which we don't agree with. Being faithful to one partner in marriage isn't really an important issue for most of the African males, even when they've been educated in Britain like Wil has. The women here also accept extra marital relationships and other wives. Women here still have little or no status. Women's rights are unheard of here as yet. Perhaps one day it will change.

'When, like you two, you marry across ethnic boundaries, one of you has to compromise. In some relationships it might be a religious compromise. If you'd stayed in Nottingham, it would likely have been Wil who'd conform to British behaviour, where monogamy is the accepted norm. But you've moved here and it looks as though you're going to have to fall in line with the local tribal laws and that means Wil can quite easily take more than one wife.

'I'm so sad for you. You don't deserve this. I hate seeing you hurt like this. I've never been in such a situation myself, so I really can't give you first-hand advice. I've never had any problems like this with John, but look at poor Marie. She's got those three lovely little girls and still Ron would run after anything in a skirt. Haven't you noticed how he ogles at you? So you see thoughts of infidelity aren't confined to Africans, there's plenty of it going on amongst the Brits as well. I know it doesn't help you at the moment, but it's a fact.'

'What would you do, Judy, if you were me?'

'That's not easy, but since you ask, let me give you the benefit of what I have to say. I think you've done the best possible thing by ignoring it for the time being. If it's possible, try and ignore it and see how things develop. You're not being threatened physically nor will he run off and leave you destitute. Life will continue as before, except that you know what's going on. Up to now you were quite happy and blissfully ignorant of what was taking place.'

'I wish you weren't going so soon. I'll have no one to talk to when you're away. That'll be the hardest for me.'

'Yes, this has come up at a bad time, but try not to tell any of the others here. They gossip enough as it is. Don't give them anything to add to it.'

'Do you think I should let Wil know that I'm aware of what's going on?'

'That's tricky. If you say you know then he might take it as a sign of acceptance and it may become an overt relationship with her. He's still trying to keep it from you. If you can, I'd say nothing if I were you. It means he's got to work on keeping it from you still.'

'I'm in such a weak position as well. I can't very well blow up and threaten to leave because I've nowhere to go and he knows that.'

The rainy season arrived with its breathtaking displays of electrical thunderstorms signalling the end of the intense drought of the dry season. The oppressive dry heat of the Harmattan winds blowing down from the Sahara in the north was reduced somewhat, but the humidity increased and the roads, as usual, turned to thick, deep mud interspersed with enormous potholes. The servants suffered their annual bouts of fever. Otherwise life carried on as normally as possible at the Sankoli compound. During August, the month of the heaviest rains, it was quite common to be enshrouded in a huge blanket of white hot mist in the hills surrounding the Club school room.

Milton was so surprised when he encountered his first shower of rain. There was a look of bewilderment on his little face, then he started looking all around to see if he could find the culprit he thought was showering him with water. He couldn't understand water coming from the sky! Fiona had to laugh out loud, he was so comical. He got some plastic cups and wanted to play with the rainwater dropping down from the roof into the open concrete drain surrounding the house. He'd not remembered the last rains when he was a baby.

Judy's leave came and went as did that of some of the staff and children at the mine. The only constant at the school was 'Miss Fiona'. Between her work and Milton she was happy and she became more and more tied up with her own pursuits. Her life became a routine of days and weeks slipping past in a state of predictability. Deep down, she was experiencing the first cracks of silent inner turmoil. She tried to block out Wil's relationship with Kissie and ignored the long working hours they spent together both at the surgery and out on social functions. She pleaded she was either tired or busy when family outings were arranged and at bedtime she frequently turned in before Wil and conveniently pretended to be asleep when he joined her.

On the surface she tried to maintain a lively disposition, but underneath it all she nursed the bitterness and sorrow of his betrayal and unfaithfulness with Kissie. She was suspicious and edgy when they stayed late at Meynard's place, but she contained her innermost fears and thoughts. A confrontation with Wil might only upset the household harmony which existed.

Her sexual relationship with Wil was severely affected by her feelings about him. He tried to persuade her to maintain their sexual relationship. Fiona felt that if the three of them could have been together without Kissie and Mama Nkozi things might have been different, but she knew that was impossible. She knew that any conflict between herself and Wil would spill over to the others and upset the equilibrium, which would only increase her own tension, not relieve it. She'd never been able to cope with any form of unpleasantness. One of the lessons she had learned from extended family life was tolerance of others and their failures and the ability to overcome her own personal weaknesses. She felt as though she was coping well with the situation by ignoring it, but it was taking its toll on her emotionally.

Her friendship with Judy and the women at the mine developed and she realised how fortunate she'd been to be offered the job. Judy had seen Jane settled into zoo life and had spread the word around that she'd be willing to accept another chimpanzee orphan. John was away most of the week, returning usually only at weekends because he was working up in the north of the country around Sefadu. Judy did have an opportunity to move with him nearer to where he worked but she would have been without any female company so she preferred to remain on the mine.

A new extension to the Sankoli compound was built comprising a cottage of two bedrooms and bathroom. This separate accommodation was officially for Regina and her children, but it was used also as the guesthouse for the friends and relations who often stayed with them. Kissie moved to the bedroom next to Mama Nkozi, which had been Regina's room and Milton got his own room next to Fiona's, which Kissie had previously occupied. At Christmas Lahai could share Milton's bedroom and Poppy and Priscilla would have the second bedroom in the new guesthouse.

Fiona made curtains for the guesthouse windows, choosing a deep pink flowery pattern for the girls' room. Mama Nkozi brought home some bright yellow cotton with a Donald Duck pattern on it for Milton's new room and Fiona made it up with matching bedcovers for both Milton and Lahai.

Christmas 1962 approached with the usual build up in anticipation of the festivities. Fiona had the children at school making paper chains and decorations to brighten the Club. She even decorated the living room at home and put up a token Christmas tree using a branch. When the girls arrived from Freetown they were delighted and she got them to help make coloured bows of crepe paper to add to the decorations on the tree. Milton was now a very lively twenty-two-month old. He was in his element at having so much attention from Poppy, Priscilla and Lahai. Regina had brought up with her what old toys Lahai no longer needed which included an old Triang tricycle. Lahai was now five. Milton was treated as the baby and was usually given much of his own way as a result.

'He's only little, let him play with it,' was how Regina tackled squabbling between the two boys. The tricycle brought out the worst of behaviour in the two of them. Lahai, who was too big for the tricycle, suddenly resented it belonging to Milton and insisted on spending nearly all his time on the trike, while Milton hung on to the back of the seat whining and stamping his feet in a tantrum. He asserted himself by lying on the floor and thrashing out his arms and legs in rage. He was just starting to speak, but only single words and he loudly called, 'Mine!' as he pulled at the back of the trike, and 'Bad, Lahai!'

'You know, Lahai hasn't looked at that trike in years,' Regina told Fiona.

'Don't worry about that. Milton's getting too much of his own way and it's time he learned he's got to give in at times. Even the boys around the house give in to him and it's not doing him any good. He's got to be brought up to learn to share and to discover that the world doesn't revolve round him. Having Lahai around will help teach him he can't have everything he wants. A bit of competition and sharing is what he needs. The girls also give in to him just because he's the baby. I see by these tantrums he's starting to try to assert himself over us all.'

'What he needs is a little brother,' declared Regina. 'That would sort him out, don't you think?'

'I don't think there's much chance of that now.'

'I would say there's no chance going by your behaviour,' Wil accusingly interrupted.

When Regina got Fiona to herself that night she cautiously asked, 'Is everything all right with you and Wil? Did I put my feet in it this afternoon?'

'I'm afraid you did! We seem to be going through a bit of a problem of late.'

'Do you want to tell me?'

'Well, he's carrying on still with Kissie I've discovered and I can't handle it.'

'Oh! Enough said!' was Regina's short reply. It seemed as though she didn't want to involved once she grasped the problem.

Mama Nkozi organised a large party of local friends for Christmas Eve, so Fiona declined the mine invitation to their traditional dinner. Preparation for the party occupied the four women for the best part of two days. They were in a lively mood and all of them were looking forward to the celebrations. Wil and Brima added to the decorations which Fiona had made and they strung up coloured bulbs on the veranda. Everything was ready for a truly enjoyable evening. Mama Nkozi was at her happiest when all the family was around her. She thrived on company and was well suited to organising such social events. The house was alive with chatter and laughter as all their friends gathered to spend the evening with them.

The party was such a success! Everybody was in a gay mood and the food and drink heightened the pleasure of the evening. The children were too excited by the preparations to go to bed early and were allowed to stay up until it was evident that they were exhausted. Milton fell asleep in Fiona's arms by eight o'clock and she carefully transferred him to his bed. Lahai followed later but Poppy and Priscilla, now eight and nine respectively, managed to spin out the evening until well after ten o'clock.

The chairs in the large room were pushed against the walls and the musicians started playing what instruments they'd brought along with them, and singing and dancing commenced. At midnight they toasted in Christmas Day and immediately thereafter Wil announced that they all toast Kissie who would be giving birth to a baby in July. Cheering and clapping followed as they all toasted her.

Fiona was thunderstruck. She felt weak and slightly sick. She backed into the nearest chair whilst the music started up again and dancing continued. Kissie was surrounded by a group of women congratulating her and she looked radiantly happy. An arm went round Fiona's shoulder as she sat there in numbed confusion. She hadn't seen Regina approach her.

'Come, Fiona, let's go to my room,' she gently whispered as she steered her out of the room, across the compound to the guesthouse. There they sat on the bed.

'I thought you were imagining it when you told me earlier. I didn't really believe you. When did you find out?'

'Quite a while ago.'

'Does Mama know?'

'Well, she does now.'

'I think it's a bit cowardly of him to take advantage of tonight to announce it before any of us knew.'

'Regina, how could he humiliate me like this in front of everybody? Why couldn't he have told me himself instead of doing it this way?'

'I expect he thought that this way you won't create a scene, which of course you haven't, and it was such an easy way out of dealing with it.'

'They're all out there cheering and happy, but how does he think I feel? I'll never be able to face all these folk again.'

'There's no shame here in having more than one wife, you know. I'm just surprised at Wil. None of these people here tonight will consider that you've been slighted. It's the culture and tradition here. They'll expect you to be happy also. In fact Wil will have more standing in the local community as a result. They will expect you to accept it and they wouldn't understand any feeling of animosity or shame on your part.'

'But where I come from this isn't acceptable. Yes, it does happen, I'm not denying that, but it's not socially accepted. It's a sign of the breakdown of a relationship not a cause for celebration.'

'I'm surprised Wil has done this, I must admit. I thought that all his years of education and working abroad, he'd be more influenced by Western standards. You do know, don't you, that Kissie was supposed to be his wife under our family customs?'

'Yes, I found that out... and I also found out they've been having a relationship together, but I've never said anything. Maybe I've been behaving a bit like an ostrich and burying my head in the sand and not facing reality these last few months.'

'Kissie's always considered him as her property and it must have been a setback to her when he married you. You must accept there's no moral code on her part to accept you as his only wife and she's no doubt been very keen to encourage him at every opportunity.'

'We can't blame it all on Kissie, you know. It takes two to tango. She didn't force him against his will, we can be sure of that.'

'Come, let's go back and join the party.'

'No, I can't face them all now.'

'Yes, you can and must. Rise above all this for tonight and I'll promise you we'll have a family meeting after breakfast tomorrow, even though it's Christmas Day.'

They returned to the party. If they'd been missed, nobody said so. Fiona drank little alcohol normally, but she made her way to the bottle of whisky on the drinks table and took a generous measure and topped her glass up with Sprite.

'Come, let's dance,' Wil whispered to her as he slipped his arm round her waist, having come up from behind her. 'Put your drink down and get it later.'

'Congratulations to the proud father-to-be are in order I believe?'

'Thank you, my darling. I trust that's not a note of sarcasm I detect. You know it doesn't become you.'

'Wil, how could you do this to me? What have I done to deserve this?'

'Come now, don't let's be dramatic about it. It's not going to affect your status any,' he softly replied.

'Status! You've the cheek to talk about status when you've got no morals whatsoever. I thought you loved me.'

'Of course I love you, for what it's worth. Let's not have a scene when everybody's enjoying themselves. You're enjoying yourself as well, aren't you?'

'I was until midnight. I can't understand or condone your behaviour.'

'Oh you and your Western puritanical values. You're living in Africa now, my darling.'

'Don't "darling" me and treat me like something you've bought and now want to discard. How would you feel if I took up with somebody else?'

'My sweet, don't you know the rules for unfaithful wives here? The village chief would sentence you to a beating. Now you wouldn't like that, would you?' he chuckled.

'I'm going to bed now. I'm not taking any more of your behaviour – and don't bother me tonight – you're not sharing my bed again.'

'Tut, tut, we're cross, are we?'

The liquor and bravado of being surrounded by friends gave him the courage to confront her with the truth. She turned on her heel and went to bed, bolting the door. She remembered that he could gain entrance to the bedroom through the joint bathroom which separated Milton's bedroom from theirs. She'd bolted the door more as a gesture of rage and hurt so that he would get the message if he tried the bedroom door.

She lay in bed feeling devastated by the night's event. Eventually anger subsided and she wept. The party continued in full swing and to the background of the lively music she fell asleep come time. She woke in the morning to the sound of him opening the underwear drawer for clean clothes. Once dressed he went and got Milton and lifted up the mosquito net and dropped him onto the bed with her. He sat on the side of the bed and said, 'Merry Christmas, darling!'

She ignored him.

'Fiona, don't let's be silly about this. You're getting it all out of proportion. You know you're still my "number one". Can't you be happy for Kissie's sake?'

She decided to keep calm and think things out before she said anything. She didn't want to explode. 'I'd better get up and help with the clearing up. Is there an awful mess through there?'

'It's mostly clearing up dirty glasses and putting things back into place. Where're Milton's clothes and I'll dress him.'

At the breakfast table there was a distinct atmosphere. The children, unaware of any tension, were a welcome diversion and stilted conversations were made relating to the success of the party. Fiona remained quiet. When Kelly served coffee and started to clear the breakfast plates away Regina said, 'You children go away and play outside for a while. There's a tin of biscuits over there. Fetch them and go down to the compound and share them with the children there. Everybody else, please, remain at the table. There's the matter of last night's announcement to be discussed.'

'What do you mean by that?' Wil looked up and squared himself with determination on his chair.

They were all tense and sitting upright.

'I can't see there's anything to add or discuss,' Wil continued. 'Kissie's pregnant and that's that. Can't you all be good enough to congratulate her?'

'Of course we're all very happy for her, but that's not the issue. Don't you think you could have told us before you announced it to the world? Didn't you have any thought for Fiona's feelings whatsoever? Did you know about this, Mama?'

'No, Regina, I didn't. Last night was the first I heard of it.'

Everyone started to chip in and the conversation got confused and more heated and then Fiona broke down.

'Quiet all of you!' Mama Nkozi raised her voice authoritatively. 'Stop all this fighting. What would your dear Papa have thought of all this? Show some respect for him.'

Fiona did wonder at that moment what showing respect to old Papa, now long since dead, had to do with Kissie being pregnant.

'Let's behave with some dignity. It's Christmas Day as well. Shame on you all. What's done is done and as a family we stick together and behave accordingly. It's come to us as a surprise and the two of you should have told us first. Now that we all know, we're all very happy and it'll be such a joy to have another baby around.'

'Mama, how can you say that when Fiona's feeling hurt and humiliated? She's not used to these standards where she comes from.'

'Now, Fiona, my dear, you mustn't be unhappy and upset. You'll get over it and once the baby's born you also will be pleased, just as Kissie was for you when Milton came along. Look how we all love and cherish him, don't we? We mustn't spoil the holidays and celebrations by petty quarrelling. Brima, make yourself useful, go and get some sherry and we'll toast the forthcoming event and show how pleased we all are.'

Brima, who'd remained silent throughout, scuttled off to the sideboard and hastily poured six small sherries and Mama Nkozi duly toasted Kissie. Fiona put on a brave face and joined in. She thought resentfully that Kissie looked like the cat who'd got the cream. Well, in some ways she had.

The next couple of days saw surface harmony restored and it would have been difficult for any outsider to detect any underlying strain. Wil shared the bed with Fiona again but she coldly turned her back on him, clinging precariously onto the edge of her side of the bed. She remained aloof from all attempts of his to engage her in conversation when they were alone.

Chapter Fifteen

On Friday morning, the twenty-eighth of December, around eleven, Poppy came screaming up the road in a highly hysterical state. Following closely behind her was a bewildered Priscilla and Lahai. Brima was first to reach Poppy and she was yelling out, 'Milton, Milton, they've taken Milton away!' and she was pointing down the road. They all rushed round her and Brima was trying to calm her down and get her to speak coherently.

Fiona immediately realised Milton wasn't with them and she started to run down the road looking for him. Instinct told her something serious was amiss. Wil overtook her and together they ran the extent of the track to the main road. There was no sign of him or anybody else whatsoever. Fiona, in a frenzy by then, started to call out his name.

'Let's go back and find out what exactly Poppy was trying to say. He's obviously not down here.' Wil was also obviously in a state of panic by then. They ran together back to the house and Brima had at last managed to get the crying child to tell him that they had been playing and going down the road, all four of them together. Poppy and Priscilla were racing to see who could get to the road first and they were giving the boys piggy-backs. Halfway there Lahai needed to go to the toilet and Priscilla had stopped to let him 'pee' at the roadside. Poppy and Milton raced on ahead and reached the junction first. She was waiting at the side of the road for the other two losers to catch them up when two men on bicycles came along.

They dismounted when they got to Poppy and asked her if Milton was a 'boy piccaninny' and when she told them he was, one of them had grabbed Milton from her back and the other man threw her into the bushes at the roadside. When she managed to get up and back onto the road, the two of them were cycling along the road away from her with Milton.

'Get into the Land Rover,' Wil ordered Brima. 'We'll go after them.'

'I'm coming as well.'

'No, you stay behind and calm down Poppy. Quick, find out which direction the men were travelling in. Find out if they were going towards Kenema or Hangha.'

Fiona rushed inside and quickly asked the confused and distressed Poppy if she could tell her which direction the men were going in. After a while she concluded by Poppy's description of the events that they were cycling away to her left, so they must have been heading in the Hangha direction. She ran outside and jumped into the Land Rover.

'I've got to come with you. He's my son after all as well as yours,' she insisted. 'By what I can make out from Poppy they were going in the Hangha direction, but she's very confused and sore after being thrown around.'

The three of them set off and turned left onto the Hangha road at the junction. They reached Hangha village and continued beyond onto Mano Junction without success. They turned round and came back into Hangha where they stopped and asked if anybody had seen two men on bicycles with a small boy. They drew a blank. The road was deserted. On their return journey Wil drove very slowly so they could scour both sides of the road, Fiona watching one side and Brima the other.

They reached home about two hours later. All the others surrounded the Land Rover as it drew up to the house, eagerly hoping for news that they had found him safe.

The realisation that he'd gone suddenly hit them all. Fiona dissolved into a flood of tears. Kissie and Mama Nkozi also broke down. The three children became distressed and Regina took her two outside to occupy them, while Kissie and Brima tended to Poppy, who was still sobbing uncontrollably as a result of her alarming experience and pain. Her body was bruised from the rough handling she'd experienced at the hands of one of the kidnappers.

Wil gently led Fiona inside and sat down on the couch with her.

'Why do you think they've taken him? What would they want with him?' she cried gently. 'Why would they want a little boy? Was there any significance in them asking if he was a boy? Do you think they'll hold him to ransom and demand money?'

'I don't know, I really don't know,' replied Wil solemnly. 'You stay here and Brima and I'll go and report it to the Kenema police, then we must search along the road again for him in case he's been left wandering about on his own somewhere.'

All work had ceased on the compound and all the staff and their families gathered round the kitchen area to find out what they could as the news of the child's disappearance became known. They talked amongst each other in hushed voices and an aura of fear surrounded them.

Wil returned with two policemen about forty minutes later. A further two policemen had been sent out along the road which they'd already searched. The police questioned Poppy and took down what details she could give them. She was quite distraught by the events and was obviously afraid that she would be blamed and punished for the incident. The incident had occurred so quickly and there was her confusion when she'd been roughly thrown into the bushes and got entangled in the undergrowth. Luckily her only injuries were minor scratches and bruises. There was also the possibility that in her confusion the two men had actually taken off in the opposite direction towards Kenema and not towards Hangha.

Fiona behaved mechanically. She answered the questions put to her by the policemen, giving an exact description of what Milton was wearing and provided them with the most recent photo they had of him.

'Do you think they will hold him and demand money for his release?' she asked one of the policemen.

He thought it was possible, though unlikely. He had never come across a case of abduction in all his fifteen years in the force. He said that he'd no reason to believe that the culprits knew who the child was. He assumed that the pair had not been lying in wait for the children. On the face of it they had taken Milton on the spur of the moment and it did not seem to have been premeditated.

Wil came and sat with Fiona after the police had gone and also broke down in tears. Brima came over to him and took him by the arm and said, 'Come, let's get all the available folk on the compound and search along the roadside again. Let's make the most of the daylight while we can, just in case he's left wandering around on the road somewhere. If we do something positive to occupy us, then I think that will help us all.'

Naturally everybody wanted to help. Fiona said she also wanted to go. She felt as if she'd go mad if she was left at home helplessly wondering where he was. The party they made up was about thirty strong and they systematically and slowly covered both sides of the road in search of any clues, beating down some of the dense undergrowth as they went along.

About four o'clock that afternoon a police Land Rover approached them from Hangha and Wil went over to speak to them. He nodded and came straight over to Fiona, put his arm round her and simply said, 'We can stop looking now. They've found him just this side of Hangha.'

'Where is he?' She frantically looked up into his face.

'Darling, you're going to have to be very brave... he's no longer alive. They've got his body in the back of the Land Rover. I'll take you back home now and arrange for all the others to be taken home as well. Then I'll have to go to the police station again to officially identify him.'

'I want to see him and go with him,' she pleaded.

'No, it's not advisable. Believe me, darling. He's gone now. Just you remember him as he was this morning, a happy little boy. You remember him like that.'

'What happened to him? Did they say?'

'I'll find all that out once I've taken you back home.'

She didn't remember much of the short journey home. She was distraught and on the verge of hysteria. There was no need to tell the others at home the outcome of the search. It was evident by the distress of everybody returning. Only the details were unknown. Wil and Brima weren't gone more than an hour. The servants all came past to offer their sympathy. The compound was gripped in grief and the women started to wail eerily outside. The haunting noise they made continued most of the night. Brima and

Regina took command of the household for the remainder of that day. Although the three children didn't totally understand, the atmosphere of sadness and all the weeping subdued and confused them. They wanted to know what was happening around them and eventually the whole family sat down and talked and discussed it until they were exhausted.

Wil and Brima told them that Milton had been killed by a blow to the head. An examination revealed that this was the injury that had presumably killed him. The most distressing part of it however was that his genitals had been removed. The police had told them that this action was consistent with one or two other cases they'd dealt with. According to them the genitals were required as some kind of offering or sacrifice to the spirits. A witch doctor would perform certain rituals and the genitals held some potent magical power to make the spell successful. The police had a theory that the crime could be linked to the diamond trade. When diamond diggers had worked some time without success, then they became desperate and would pay a witch doctor to cast a magic spell and perform a dance to appease the spirits responsible. Thereafter they expected their luck to change and find diamonds. They said they would be making enquiries of the local diamond diggers and they would concentrate their investigations initially in the alluvial diamond digging area. The police revealed that the chances of finding out much were not high because of the superstitious nature of the people, many of whom believed in the extraordinary powers of sacrificing parts of the human body. This made progress extremely difficult. They confirmed that any investigations which had magic or 'juju' implications were hampered by silence. Fear of being 'cursed' made people terrified to speak out even if they did know something.

Fiona could hardly believe all this talk of medieval witchcraft having been responsible for killing her son was really true. To think that such a hideous crime could take place in the twentieth century sounded like some Robinson Crusoe story when the cannibals ate their prisoners.

The children ate that night, but for the adults coffee was the only requirement. Nobody had an appetite they were so distraught. Shortly after seven that evening Meynard was the first of a flood of callers to arrive. The news had travelled fast. Wil dispensed sedatives to Fiona and she fell into a deep daze. She felt as if she wasn't present, akin to an out-of-body experience and was looking down on the sorrowful group. It was like watching an uncomfortable stage play which once over, would allow her to get up and leave and return to normality. Later on that night Wil sedated Fiona further and she collapsed into oblivion.

Milton was buried next day, which is the normal custom in Sierra Leone because of the climatic conditions. Fiona was too ill to attend. She remained in bed all that Saturday and Sunday in a highly emotional state, controlled only by sedatives. She drifted in and out of various stages of consciousness. When she became lucid she wept uncontrollably. All of the three women in turn came and sat with her in an effort to comfort and console her, but she rejected any of their attempts. Kissie and Mama Nkozi had both played such an important role in Milton's upbringing and were also grief-stricken.

On the Sunday night Wil tried to reach Fiona. He pleaded with her to help him in his sorrow. He reminded her that he too had lost his son and he was grieving deep down as much as she was. She was weak and exhausted, partly from not eating and partly because of all the crying she'd done.

'Let's try and cope with this together. We should give each other strength to carry on and handle the tragedy,' he begged.

'I don't want to carry on. I've got nothing left to carry on for,' she replied bitterly.

'Look, my darling, we're all here to support you. Please give us a chance. You've got to get up tomorrow and make a bit of an effort.'

'I can't face anybody now. I just want to die. Just give me enough tablets to do it and you'll be rid of me as well.'

Wil couldn't make any progress; she seemed in such deep shock and depression. He decided to dispense tranquillisers for her and administer them himself in view of her poor state of mind. Next day he persuaded her to rise, bath and join the others for breakfast. He'd told her that Poppy wasn't coping very well since the incident and was suffering from a guilt complex. She'd convinced herself that she was responsible for Milton's death and was fearful that the family were blaming her and now no longer loved her.

'Won't you try and speak to Poppy? You and her have always been close friends. Can't you reassure her that we don't blame her and that it wasn't her fault? She needs to know that you are still her friend and still love her. Won't you please try, please, sweetie. She'll be going back to Freetown with them at the end of the week. Make up with her somehow. I don't think it's a good idea that she stay on longer here on her own under the circumstances. She'd be better off out of this atmosphere for the remainder of the holidays.'

'It's not her fault, it's my fault he's gone. If I'd been looking after him properly then this would never have happened.'

'You know that's ridiculous. You know you're not to blame. Nobody's to blame. There's no use after something has happened starting on with 'if only'. It was just one of those terrible coincidences that he just happened to be in the right place at the wrong time. We've got to accept it was a hideous accident which couldn't have been foreseen or prevented. God must have had a reason for taking him from us. Try and think that he's happy somewhere beautiful like heaven now, living a better life than this earthly one.'

'To hell with God and wanting him,' she rasped angrily. 'God should think of me down here then, suffering. He should take me as well as I don't want to be without Milton. I want him more than God ever did. God could have taken dozens of those starving sickly children out there instead.'

'He'll likely take them all in time too,' Wil replied, realising it was too soon to try to reason with her.

Fiona did feel somewhat better after bathing and dressing and managed to eat some breakfast with the others. Everything around was so normal, the conversation and the children's excited chatter. She knew that they were all making an effort to be extra friendly with her and attempting to include her in the conversation. It was as though she was surrounded by an invisible wall which they were all desperately trying to penetrate to reach her, but she was hiding within that wall, neither prepared to be reached nor wanting to step out from it.

Before breakfast had been completely cleared away the Geological Survey Land Rover arrived with John and Judy. News had reached them of the tragedy, though garbled and incomplete. They all sat down in the room together with John and Judy and took them through the heartbreaking sequence of events. Fiona remained calm and tearless throughout, listening again to the familiar horrible tale which when related, sounded like an evil version of some fairy story, without a happy ending. The others seemed to gain strength by virtue of simply talking through the happenings. Fiona knew how sad Judy felt, and recognised her inability to do or say anything which could alleviate her pain. Once they had exhausted their theories and conclusions on what had happened, how and why, John and Judy left. Judy had asked Fiona if she would like to come and spend a few days with her, but she declined the offer. However, she agreed to go over on Thursday for the day. That was the day Regina and family would be leaving for home. That would save her being on her own also when the others were at work. Wil suggested she stay over one night and he would collect her on Friday evening.

It was with a certain degree of relief that Fiona waved goodbye to Regina, Brima and the children, and she set off to see Judy. Wil had arranged to go late to surgery that morning because he wanted to drive Fiona himself. Fiona did acknowledge that he was also grieving and that he was genuinely concerned about her, but she couldn't respond to his approaches of loving or friendship. He had tried to embrace her at night in bed, but she turned her back firmly on him and rejected all his attempts, even though they weren't necessarily sexual.

She felt angry and hurt over Kissie's pregnancy, though it was of such minor importance to her since the death of Milton. She felt an inner emptiness as if part of her had also died with Milton. She was deeply unhappy and sorry for herself and wasn't at all interested in stories of others who had undergone and suffered similar tragedies.

Judy was awaiting her arrival. Wil stayed long enough to have some coffee before returning. He told Judy that he'd given Fiona tranquillisers to take to help her cope and left a couple of sleeping tablets also. Judy suggested he collect her the following evening and come for dinner and they could chat or play cards afterwards. She promised to make her speciality – Cornish pasties – and recommended he take his Rennies with him just in case!

All that day they talked and talked. Fiona managed to pour out some of her inner thoughts and doubts to Judy. She told her about the Kissie pregnancy and how she'd been hurt and humiliated by the way Wil had made the announcement at the party.

'There's nothing left for me here now. I've died inside and feel I can't face any more.'

'I do know some of what you're feeling. You know twenty-one years ago I also had a baby taken from me. I'd complications during the labour and birth and my baby was stillborn as a result. You've suffered a crueller blow because you had Milton for nearly two years and he was a real little person, whereas I never knew my baby and what it was like to look after and care for her. I was still devastated though, so much to look forward to and then after all the complication and pain I ended up with nothing. Not only did I have no baby, but I was never able to have another one, so I do share something with you. Jane was the nearest to a child I've ever had, and it may sound ridiculous to you, but I've felt a great sense of loss now I've no longer got her. I know others used to scoff at me, but she did give me so much pleasure.'

'You know, Fiona, you've been stretched too far emotionally recently, but you're young and resilient beneath all this. Time will help and you will heal emotionally. Perhaps never totally in Milton's case, but sufficiently to carry on with your life. Eventually you'll remember him with love and be grateful that you had him and enjoyed so much love and happiness from him in his short life. Don't be afraid to talk about him. Because he's no longer here doesn't mean he didn't exist. Don't be ashamed to cry and mourn him. Mourning and crying are both part of death and dying. It's not a weakness or something to be ashamed of. Just try and hold on to reality in the meantime to keep you going.'

'What do you think I should do about Wil and Kissie now? He's basically announced publicly that they are lovers.'

'What a pity you've had to cope with this as well just now. What a shame you're so far from home and have no parental support to turn to. I'm sure both Mama Nkozi, Kissie and Wil, despite everything, are honestly concerned and recognise your unhappiness. I would try to carry on with life as best as you can for some time to give yourself a chance to heal a bit, then see how things are. For the meantime, I suggest you take each day as it comes. You know, my dear, you're always welcome here with me at any time. You know I care dearly for you. If my daughter had lived I'd have wished her to be just like you. Mind, I'm not so sure that I'd have been any different from your mother though. I don't think I'd have been able to cope too well with accepting Wil as my son-in-law, even though I both like and respect him.'

Even Fiona had to laugh a little at that. 'I can always trust you to say what you think, can't I? That's where you're different from Mum. I think part of the problem was she couldn't accept that I was an adult and needed to be treated as such.'

'Will you want to take school again on Monday or do you want to cancel for another week?'

'No, I'll start again on Monday as planned. I don't feel up to it in some ways, but if I can keep busy it will help me to take my mind off everything. It will help fill some of the emptiness I'm left with. It also means I won't be left in the house all day on my own. The only thing I'm worried about is how to cope with the children's questions if they ask.'

'They all know already of course, but children are very resilient you know. They can accept death sometimes better than adults. If any of them do ask, try and be honest with them and even talk about it with them if you feel you can. I think it's a good idea that you start back on Monday.'

'I don't know what I'd have done without the mine to come to and everybody here. I'd have been so much more alone if it weren't for you.'

'Well, that's what friends are for after all. Tomorrow we'll make pasties and then in the afternoon we should go down to the pool. I think it'll be good for you to see the others and overcome the initial awkwardness that you'll feel. That's what I found so difficult when I lost the baby – facing people. I was frightened I couldn't cope. They all want to see you anyway. They've all been so upset and sad for you. John won't be out tomorrow either so he can come as well. He's got paperwork to catch up on he says.'

The new school year of 1963 started with packing away the Christmas decorations and hanging up a new calendar. Fiona thought wistfully as she hung it up that a new year must surely have better things in store for her than the last one. She spent most of her energy on the class and the six pupils. What spare time she had she sewed and read. Outwardly she appeared to be coping well, but inwardly she battled to come to terms with losing Milton. Wil and her were not on friendly terms. He tried and tried to reach out to her, but to no avail. She remained cool and distant in bed and it became accepted now that he remain on his designated side of the bed. Her capacity to love had died just as surely as Milton had. She was unable to show any interest in Kissie's forthcoming child. She'd intimated in a disinterested tone that Wil could move into Kissie's bedroom if he wanted to. She wasn't able to muster any enthusiasm to even get angry at the situation any more. Wil, in desperation, suggested he take a week off and they could go and spend some time in Freetown with Regina. She could go to the beach and the shops, but she refused. Her main interest now was her work and her close relationship with Judy. She was leading her own independent life. The moral support which normally should have come from her husband during her mourning period was now coming from Judy's friendship. Judy knew that from her attitude, Wil was slowly losing Fiona. She'd lost that sparkle of enthusiasm which came from being in love that she'd originally had. Judy worried about what would become of Fiona. She herself would be moving away to another of John's overseas assignments and who would befriend her then? Perhaps she'd revive her love for Wil once she started to feel less grief inside.

At the end of June, another devastating blow was dealt to Fiona. The mine was to close down at the end of August and the ex-pat staff contracts would be terminated. For Fiona that meant her lifeline would go. The job and her contact with the mine was basically what had kept her going since Milton's death.

The announcement was such a bitter blow. It transpired that the mine had negotiated, many years previously, a deal with the Government which enabled it to rail ore to Freetown at a very attractive low cost. That contract was due to expire and despite attempts by the London office to negotiate similar terms for a further contract, the Government had upped the price considerably. The world price of chromite was already low and the increased haulage cost meant that the extraction of ore was no longer a financially viable business venture. The staff would be released from their contracts and could start to return to their homes during the month of August.

The future of the mine would be held in the hands of three local employees who would remain on a monthly basis until such time as a sale of all, or most, of the moveable equipment could be negotiated. The three remaining employees were all bachelors. John and Judy would still be able to rent their accommodation from the mine until such time as they were due to leave, which was July. John's surveying and mapping assignment would be completed by then, after which he would be transferred to another country.

For the mine employees the shock announcement was tinged with a degree of excitement. They could look forward to going home soon, but for Fiona, it meant another void to be created in her already lonely life.

Wil was disturbed and distressed by the news. He realised the implications. He knew that Fiona's only support was coming from her work with the mine children. Once that was gone, he was worried how she would cope. He suggested she open a little school in Kenema for some of the local children, but there was a substantial language barrier. Very few children spoke anything but their local languages. Her best chance of work would be in Freetown and that wasn't the answer.

Wil was at a loss on how to handle Fiona. He'd lie in bed at night next to her and try to get her to even talk to him. He'd at one time suggested she should try to become pregnant again. Her responses to him were listless, the fighting spirit within her had gone; she wasn't even angry with him any more. He'd suggested that once Kissie's baby arrived she'd feel different and could help look after it, but she made it clear she wanted no part in the child's upbringing and they would have to find a nursemaid to look after the child when Kissie returned to work. At one stage he got angry with her and accused her of being selfish and inconsiderate, but she merely shrugged her shoulders and admitted she probably was.

Classes at the mine ended at the end of July and over the next month all the families packed up and left. John and Judy left early in July, planning to be in Freetown for three weeks prior to flying to England.

Life at the Sankoli household wasn't unpleasant or unhappy, just somewhat strained. The excitement which had surrounded Fiona's pregnancy two years ago was distinctly lacking for Kissie. Kissie herself was radiantly happy and gave birth to a son of nearly ten pounds in weight on the twentieth of July.

Wil was obviously happy with his new son. The night the baby was born Mama Nkozi organised a couple of goats to be barbecued and friends gathered to celebrate, just as they did when Fiona had given birth to Milton. Fiona did feel happy for Kissie and did help her with little Wilberforce, as he was named. Kissie asked Fiona if she could name the baby Wilberforce Milton. Fiona agreed. She would have liked to have refused, but realised that it would have been petty of her to do so. Kissie had loved and missed Milton and she was in her own way seeking Fiona's acceptance of the new baby. Little Wil was so different to Milton, that it was easy for Fiona to accept him into the family.

Chapter Sixteen

Early in July, Wil suggested to Fiona that as soon as the school closed she should take a holiday. He suggested she write and ask her college friend, Judith, if she could visit her in Nottingham for a month or so. He said he felt a trip home would be the tonic she needed after the traumas of the last few months. He was sure that a complete break would make her feel her old self again.

Judith had corresponded with Fiona, though not too frequently. She had married one of the schoolteachers she worked with and they had moved to a terraced house within walking distance of the school they both taught at.

Fiona had immediately written her a short airmail letter and about three weeks later Judith replied to say they'd love to have her and looked forward to seeing her soon. Wil presented Fiona with a ticket to London and she started to feel some excitement about the prospect of returning home. She'd witnessed all the excitement of others going on holiday whilst working at the mine and now it was difficult for her to believe that at last it was her turn.

At the end of August she flew home. Wil took her to the airstrip at Kenema. The plane was late coming in from Freetown because of the rain and low cloud. She left Kenema on the internal flight two hours later than scheduled. Her departure that day was in stark contrast to her arrival there nearly three years previously. How naïve she'd been then; a young bride eagerly looking forward to her new life in Sierra Leone. How much wiser she was now. Wil kissed her gently goodbye.

'Look after yourself and enjoy yourself, my dearest,' he told her.

Brima, Regina and the three children met her from the plane. They knew the plane would be late in since it hadn't left Freetown on time that morning. Fiona and Regina talked that night, after the children were bedded, about Milton and together they relived that terrible Friday.

'Have the police made any arrests, or progress yet?'

'No, nothing. Wil gets news from them occasionally, but it seems they've come up against a brick wall. They seem to think fear and superstition prevents the natives from assisting police with any crime which has 'juju' implications. The two who took him seem to have left no clues for the police to follow up and if anybody did see them that day, they're keeping quiet.'

'You know, over these last few months, I've often thought how thankful we should be that they found his body. Can you imagine what further anguish you'd be bearing if no body had turned up and you'd never known what had become of him? I know it's only a small consolation, but at least he's still not missing.'

'Yes, I do know what you mean and I don't know how I'd have coped if he were still missing. At least I know for certain he's dead. I know how he died and also we think we know why he died. To have him disappear and be constantly looking for him and not knowing would have been more than I could have borne. Yes, I've got to be grateful that I know and I've not been left in limbo. Having to live without knowing and constantly pretending to myself that perhaps he's alive out there somewhere would be more than I could have handled. As it is, I'm still very emotionally drained. How has Poppy come out of it? Has she had any problems?'

'She seems to have got over it all now, but initially it took quite a while for her to accept it, particularly since she felt so much responsibility for it happening. Time has helped a lot and talking it over with them all and ensuring that she understood it was an accident and there wasn't any blame attached to it. She got a terrible fright because she was old enough to understand that they were wicked men.'

'She was lucky they didn't kill her as well. Maybe if she'd put up more of a struggle they might have.'

'What's going to happen now between you and Wil now that Kissie's had the baby?'

'I don't know. I honestly don't know how to handle my life any more. I'm sure Wil still cares for me, but I'm so confused emotionally I can't make any rational decisions.'

'Do you think that you could come to terms with sharing him with Kissie? I know it's not acceptable in your country, but could you continue like that? I'm sure he never intentionally wanted you to be hurt, but our men see sex and women in a different context. Here, we women are definitely second-class citizens and have very limited social status.'

'You know I'm hoping that once I get home I'll be sufficiently removed from the situation to look at it in a more objective light. I think that's the best answer I can give you for now. I seem to have lost sight of what I want and in what direction I'm going. I know of cases at home where women put up with husbands having extra-marital relationships and still stay faithful to them. I'll have to consider seriously if I can cope with and accept that kind of situation.'

Next day she flew from Lungi to Las Palmas via the Gambia. That night in the hotel in Las Palmas she was lost and lonely and sat on the bed and wept. It was the first night she'd been alone since that night in Las Palmas on her flight out. How different the circumstances had been then. How excited she'd been that night. She'd had everything to look forward to. Now she was returning with nothing. She didn't even want to venture out into the town to see the shops. She remained in her room and only went down for dinner. The bright lights of the town and the carefree holiday atmosphere didn't tempt her at all.

The second leg of the journey the following day took her to London via Lisbon. She felt quite choked up as the plane started to descend for the landing. She looked down on the neatly ordered English landscape and saw the patterns of the roads, fields, houses and gardens below. At last she was home again!

Crossing London in the underground to King's Cross, she started to regain some of the confidence she had lacked the previous evening. She made her way to St Pancras railway station and bought a ticket to Nottingham. She'd just over an hour to wait so she went to the cafeteria there and had a coffee. She'd have loved a cup of tea, but her memories of British Rail tea, made her choose coffee instead. She phoned Judith and gave her the arrival time and soon she was off on the two-hour journey north.

It was still light and that was such a thrill to experience daylight again after six o'clock. It was a warm evening, by English standards, but she didn't feel the temperature, she was too preoccupied just visually devouring the scenery as the train sped on its journey. The familiarity of the British countryside started to make her feel happier than she'd been for a long time. Perhaps Wil was right after all. A trip home was surely going to help her state of mind.

That night at Judith's, even although she'd arrived late, the two of them sat up for hours catching up on the past three years. Judith's husband, Gareth, had sat with them initially, but he crawled off to bed about midnight in need of sleep and left them still chatting excitedly.

The first week in Nottingham she spent re-exploring the town, its streets, its parks and best of all its shops. She walked everywhere and the familiar sights brought back so many memories of her college days and her courtship with Wil. In some ways nothing had changed. Some landmarks had altered, but basically Nottingham was the same place she'd left three years previously. It was Fiona who had changed. The shops and consumer goods available amazed her. Everything she could think of, and more, was available – so different to Kenema.

In the evenings Gareth, Judith and Fiona would go out, visit a pub and a couple of times they went to the cinema. She wrote Judy who was still in St Ives and within three days had a reply asking her to visit them before they left for a tour of duty to Port Louis, Mauritius at the end of September.

When she was at Judy's a letter from Wil arrived, which Judith had re-addressed.

My dearest Fiona,

I hope this letter finds you safe and happy after your journey home.

I've thought long and hard recently about our relationship and have concluded that you would be happier without me. Please be assured that I still love you dearly and want you to return to me when you can to be my wife again. If you feel that you no longer want to fulfil your duties as my wife, I will indeed be sad.

Can I ask you to think seriously and honestly about our relationship and if you feel that a parting is what you want, then I will admit adultery to make a divorce the quickest and easiest route to take.

Please let me know what you think is best.

My love to you always, Wil

Fiona handed the letter to Judy. 'I see he's sent me home to get rid of me.'

Judy read the letter, folded it and handed it back to Fiona. 'I don't think you should put it as harshly as that, Fiona. I think he's leaving you the option to decide one way or another. I'm sure he'd quite gladly have you back. What are you going to do? Will you go back now or not?'

'I'm in a total muddle. I've no other attachments either in Sierra Leone or here. I don't particularly want to turn back to what I've just left, but equally, I don't know if I've enough courage to go forward from here. My marriage is in pieces. I've failed as both a wife and mother.'

'Come now, Fiona, you can't make sweeping statements like that. You've endured so many knocks lately that your confidence has been tested to the full. You can't take all the blame for your marriage crisis. You've still got a lot of pent-up hostility in your system and that's understandable. You must realise that you and Wil are so different. It's that gap that you're finding so difficult to bridge. Your ideas and ideals over time have proved so disparate that to hold on to a harmonious marriage has proved virtually impossible. Initially the two of you spanned that gap with love and physical attraction. That's now eroded away and the gap is all that's left. Can't you just accept it like that now? Don't look for excuses to blame either him or yourself. Analysing everything in minute detail won't help to revitalise the relationship.'

The letter effectively made Fiona face that she was at a crossroads and was forcing her to make the vital, final decision. She either returned to Wil and shared him with Kissie and his mother, or she could make the break. The option was hers. It was an option she didn't want to face right there and then.

After a week in Cornwall with John and Judy she resolved to opt for divorce and not return to Sierra Leone. She'd talked at length with Judy who understood all the circumstances at first hand. Judy was also realistic and made Fiona think seriously about her future.

Did she love Wil enough to restore a sexual relationship? Could she accept and condone a continued lifetime commitment to Kissie? Could she happily remain in Kenema for the rest of her life?

Judy persuaded her not to make any hasty decision, bearing in mind that her emotional state was still suffering under the strain of Milton's death. She suggested Fiona write to her mother and see if she could at least visit and breach that gap. She felt certain that the family environment would go a long way to restoring her confidence and help heal her emotional wounds.

Fiona's mother, Jessie, was busy with the usual Monday washing when she heard the familiar flip of the letter box and the post dropping onto the floor. As a matter of routine, she dried her soapy hands on the clean towel she'd only an hour ago put on the hook at the side of the sink and passed through the living room, out into the porch and picked up the two awaiting envelopes. One was the electricity bill, which she'd been expecting. The other was in Fiona's handwriting and posted from Nottingham. She hesitated before opening it, slightly apprehensive of what it would contain. She returned to the kitchen, opened the cutlery drawer, withdrew one of the knives and carefully slit the envelope. Her heartbeat had increased, though she wasn't immediately aware of it.

Dear Mum and Dad,

I'm in Nottingham staying with Judith. Wil and I have agreed to part. I'd very much like to come and visit you both. Can I come at the weekend and stay for a week?

With love from Fiona

She was so excited. All the animosity she'd harboured over the past three and a half years since Fiona's last homecoming, started to melt away. The morning flew and the work was done twice as fast as normal. The excitement made her adrenaline flow. She was impatient now for Archie or Stanley to come home so she could share the news. First of all she'd have to reply so Fiona could get the letter Wednesday at the latest. That afternoon she wrote to her saying she must come home for as long as she liked and as soon as possible. She stamped and posted the letter straight away. Not trusting the post-box at the corner of the street, she took her letter all the way to the box at the post office to ensure it got off as fast as possible.

The back door opened shortly after Archie's van drew up at the side of the house and he'd only got his feet on the mat when he saw Jessie was standing in the kitchen waiting for him. She looked slightly harassed and agitated, so he knew some kind of problem had arisen, or some juicy piece of scandal had fallen her way during the course of the day.

'What's up then?' he asked.

'We're to have a visitor.'

'And who might that be then?'

'You'll never guess.'

'No, lass, I don't suppose I will. Best you just tell me 'cause I know you're dying to.'

'Fiona will be home at the weekend. She's in Nottingham staying with Judith. There's the letter. Read it for yourself. See what she says. I'll pour you a cup of tea and you can read it while you're drinking.'

He took off his shoes, as was the rule of the house, though he had an idea that he could have got off with it that once as Mum was in such good spirits. He sat down at the kitchen table, which was already set for tea and took the letter that she handed to him and carefully read it.

'Looks as though she's home for good as well I'd say'

'Yes, I knew that would never last. I was sure no good would come out of her marrying him.'

'Now look here, Jessie,' he carefully said. 'I don't think she's coming home to hear you say those kind of things to her. Just see that you hold your tongue this once. Let's forget all that unpleasantness and put the past behind.'

'Of course I will, don't you heed about that. It'll never be mentioned. What's done is done and now forgotten.'

The overnight train from Nottingham to Scotland brought Fiona back home again. A journey which was quite familiar from her college days. How deceptive time was. She felt it had been so long since she'd seen her parents, yet once on the journey, everything about the trip was such that it could have been last week that she'd last been there. A short bus trip took her to her home town. Nothing seemed changed as she walked down the road to the front door. Her parents were so happy to see her; her mother in particular, fussed round her. Stanley had gone to the local football match, but when he came in, it was evident he was also pleased she was home.

In the two weeks she spent at home she began to relax and was able to consider her future more rationally. Winter was drawing near and the autumn weather was turning colder. She walked the streets, seeing the stone houses and the local architecture, as for the first time. She often walked along the beach and down to the harbour and the lighthouse. Somehow she fitted in with the local people so easily. Here at home she felt part of things and part of the community.

The family naturally wanted to know about life in Africa, but never did any of them refer to her marriage to Wil. Her mother went to great lengths at the first available opportunity they were alone together, to stress that she was welcome to stay at home for as long as she liked and that the past was past and a 'closed book'. The past would never be brought up in the house again.

Fiona did feel sad to know that this was how her mother handled the less pleasant things in life. She simply pretended they never took place. She must have the ability to blot it out of her mind completely. Fiona knew that only her parents and Stanley were aware of her relationship and marriage to Wil. Stanley had been able to confirm that he'd been sworn to secrecy over the scandal. At least when neighbours and friends asked her what she'd been doing, she could honestly confirm that she'd been teaching out in West Africa. That at least was true, even though it was only a small part of the story.

Before she returned to Nottingham she met her old school-teacher, Miss MacLeod, in the butcher's shop and she asked Fiona if she would be interested in a post which was to become vacant at Christmas. She would be retiring then. Fiona had thought up till then that she would look for work in the Nottingham area. She considered it unfair to return home and live with her parents again. She felt she ought to try to be independent and make a new start to life on her own and stand on her own two feet.

'Why don't you just take it?' Stanley had wanted to know when she told him about meeting Miss MacLeod. 'You know it would be such a boost for the old lady.' He was of course referring to his mother. 'She's really eaten herself up inside over you. On the surface she's pretended she didn't care, but you should have seen the change in her when your letter came last week. Why don't you give it a chance here for a bit? You know she'll spoil you, provided you toe the line!' he laughed. 'And at least you won't be able to meet any more blacks in our town!'

'Oh, go on with you. You've still not changed, have you? I doubt if you ever will either. I can see we're going to have some job marrying you off!'

'Don't you be so sure. There's at least half a dozen of them just waiting to catch me out there, but I know where I'm well off,' he chuckled. 'By the way do you remember Isobel Stewart? She was in the class above you at school.'

'Yes, I remember her. She'd long black hair in pigtails. What about her?'

'Oh, she's just one of the ones dying to get her hands on me, but I'm keeping my options open and playing hard to get.'

'Get away with you! She'd never look at the likes of you.'

'Don't you be so sure of that.'

'What does she do now?'

'She works in Elgin now, in Austin the bakers, on South Street.'

'How long have you been going with her then?'

'Well, not seriously, but on and off for the last six months or so.'

'Has she been round to the house yet?'

'No, not yet.'

'Why don't you bring her round one night now that I'm here? I'd like to see her again.'

'I might just do that then.'

Late November Fiona returned home and in January she started work at the local school. She had instructed a firm of solicitors in Nottingham to initiate divorce proceedings and matters were left in their hands. Slowly, but surely the settling influence of her surroundings and her work absorbed all her attention and spare time. She gained strength and security from her regular routine. She was the model daughter to her parents. Mum seldom referred to her life abroad and as time went by, Fiona's loss did become less severe. She'd never ever forget her dear little son, but she did come to terms with his death gradually as the years passed.

She seldom went out socially, particularly in the first couple of years and eventually she got out of the habit of going out.

'You should be going out enjoying yourself,' her mother would sometimes lament. 'It's not natural for somebody young to be staying in all the time.'

'Where would I go now at my age?' Fiona would respond. 'If I go to the dances all the girls are about eighteen. I'd be the oldest person there!'

Stanley must have decided it was time he started to think of settling down because he was seeing more and more of Isobel Stewart. That pleased Fiona because she liked her and got on well with her. Fortunately, so did Fiona's mother. Eventually they became engaged and were married in the summer of 1966.

After the wedding Fiona spent a lot of time with Isobel and Stanley. Stanley's school-friend and work-mate, Bruce, was always around and he would make up a foursome for them to go out and about socially. They made a happy comfortable foursome. Bruce and Stanley were two of a kind and had been friends for as long back as she could remember. The two of them had got up to plenty of mischief as children and even now as adults they encouraged each other with witty repartee. Apart, without each other's moral support, they were both quite shy and sensitive.

Chapter Seventeen

'And that's about it!'

'Gosh, I'd no idea you'd been through all that. You've never ever given any hint of it.'

'No, I've tried to put it all behind me. In some ways it's been easy as it all happened so far away from here and nothing here reminds me of it. It was such a totally different life I had then. I've really got over most of it all now, but it's not a story I'm very proud of. You've got to know the truth about my past. You've got to think about it and have the option to decide if you would ever be able to accept it as part of me. It could well be that now you know all this, you can't come to terms with my past. After all I'm a divorcee. Another thing, I don't know if I can cope with the emotional side of marriage again. I find my life very "safe" the way I am.'

'Look, Fee, after what you told me last night, I thought about it most of the night as I hardly slept. It doesn't make any difference to me whatsoever what you've told me. There are very few virgins tripping down the aisle these days you know. Together I'm sure we can make a good marriage. You're surely not going to remain single and punish yourself all your life for a mistake you made when you were young? Divorce no longer holds the stigma it used to do. It's acceptable to admit your marriage wasn't a success. It doesn't have to be anybody's fault and you seem to have had the most bizarre set of circumstances to cope with. For my part, I still want to marry you. I'll wait if you want longer to think about it. What do you say to that?'

'I wish I could be sure, Bruce.'

'Sure of what?'

'Of everything I suppose.'

'That's a pretty tall order, you know! I don't think there're any guarantees with anything in life. If everybody waited until they were sure of everything they did, then I suspect nobody would take any chances and nobody would get anywhere in life. I'm not sure of anything myself come to that.'

They started to retrace their tracks along the path again and returned to the car.

'Tell you what,' he cheerfully said, 'I'll be fair with you. It's Saturday today. Why don't you think it all over seriously through the coming week? I want to marry you, make no mistake about that. I'm also prepared to wait as well if you think you could put up with me.' He held her small hand clasped firmly in his strong rough, weather-beaten hands and gently spoke with a smile on his face. 'I can't guarantee success, but I think we've got a good chance of it working out. Try and loosen up a bit. I think you're looking for problems where none exist. You're being hypersensitive. Stop punishing yourself for what's gone before. Let go of the past. Let's just face whatever the future holds. My shoulder's here to cry on any time you want. I'll not bother you during the week, but what about meeting me on Friday? We can go out and have a drink together and go to the pictures afterwards if there's anything on worth seeing. Maybe you'll be able to give me some indication of what your answer's going to be then? That a deal?'

'Suits me,' she fondly replied. 'I'll think about everything you've said and I'll give you my answer on Friday then.'

'I'll die if you turn me down, you know!' he joked.

'I'm sure you won't,' she quickly replied. 'Only your ego would be dented!'

He dropped her off that evening at home.

'Till Friday then?' He held his crossed fingers up to her as she went into the house and called out, 'Just for luck! I'll come round after work for you.'

Chapter Eighteen

It was nearing the end of the school year and Fiona was busy with student reports that week at work. She was looking forward to the summer holidays but in the forefront of her thoughts was the pressing dilemma of Bruce's proposal. She'd argued the pros and cons to herself and she was thinking that she should accept his offer. They could have a comfortable life together. With his share in the trawler he earned a good living. She admitted to herself that she didn't really want to end up an old maid. On the other hand, could she fulfil her role as a wife? Could she dare to lay herself open for perhaps another future heartache? Would it, or could it, turn out to be another hurting, painful experience? Should she perhaps opt for retaining the safety of her *status quo*? She continued to wrestle with these thoughts. Sometimes she thought she'd take the chance, other times she was too frightened to. Her feelings swung backwards and forwards like a clock's pendulum – for, against, for, against... She didn't want to face the responsibility of making the choice. She was beginning to think she'd best stall for time and ask Bruce to give her more thinking space. After all he did say he'd wait.

On the Wednesday evening of that trying week she was out in the garden with her father helping to net his raspberry canes. The berries were hanging heavy on the bushes and would soon be ripe and he didn't want the birds to get the benefit of such a good crop. It was nearly eight o'clock when Isobel arrived unexpectedly with Ian. Fiona realised immediately there was a problem as already it was past Ian's bedtime. Isobel was agitated because Stanley wasn't yet home from work. She'd not put Ian to bed, expecting him in at any time. She had become slightly worried so she'd taken a walk down to the harbour and the *Endeavour* hadn't docked, which she knew was unusual.

Mum made tea and they chatted. Dad said that they'd perhaps taken the trawler further out to sea than normal if they hadn't got a good catch and that it would take them longer to return to port. The weather was good. There hadn't been any reports of storms or squalls that day and it was after all still relatively early. There was no need to worry. The company and Dad's assurances went a long way to help Isobel. She admitted she'd just got a bit worried, especially when she was on her own.

The *Endeavour* with its crew of five had gone out the previous afternoon and they would have shot their nets before dark. Come daylight they would have hauled in their catch before returning home. Bruce's father was the skipper and he was an experienced seaman who knew the North Sea waters well. Stanley and Bruce owned a share of the trawler with him, together with two other local seamen.

Before too long Ian began to get restless and grumpy. He was overtired.

'I'll come home with you and stay until Stanley comes home,' Fiona volunteered.

'You don't mind, do you?'

'You know I don't! We'll get Ian off to bed and I'll be company for you.'

'I'll take a walk down to the harbour and see if there's any sign of them and I'll call past later,' said Dad.

'Fine, we'll see you later on then.'

They got Ian bedded and they sat and talked and the time ticked away slowly. Dad called about ten thirty but he had no news. No message had been received by anybody from the *Endeavour*'s radio. The fishermen who'd been out that day confirmed the conditions had been good. None of them had sighted the *Endeavour* that day, but she had headed out northwards on her outward journey.

Fiona stayed with Isobel all that night. As the hours slowly passed their cheerfulness faded and was replaced by anxiety. There was no point in going to bed. Sleep was impossible, so they waited and waited patiently. Fears grew with time.

Dad made a second journey down to the harbour. He was clearly ill at ease.

'What if she's disappeared?' Isobel asked Fiona.

'You mustn't think like that.'

'What else can I think?' she started to sob. 'What will we do without Stanley? What could have happened to them?'

'The sea wasn't rough so there must be some logical reason. Maybe they had some problem and have gone into another port for the night.'

'But we would have got some message by now if that's what they had done. You don't think one of them Russian submarines has got tangled up in their nets and dragged the trawler down, do you?'

'Try not to think like that, Isobel, otherwise we're both going to get upset. Why don't you go and make us some coffee? I feel a need for a caffeine boost.'

Isobel went into the kitchen to make the drinks and left Fiona alone in the lounge. She was trying to think positively, but the events were building up and she began to consider the possibility of losing both her brother and Bruce. She might never see either of them again. Tears swelled up at the thought of such a possibility and panic started to grip her.

'I can't take much more of this strain,' she cried wearily to Isobel when she brought the coffee.

'Come now, Fee, you're supposed to be here to cheer me up and now look at you.'

'Oh, Isobel, I feel so awful!'

'I know, I'm not feeling too good either. God, please make them safe,' she implored.

They sat up all night, snatching between them only a few hours of fitful dozing on the chairs. Next morning Fiona had to go to work. She didn't feel like it but once she was there the job kept her mind occupied, but she was exhausted with lack of sleep and worry.

All the fishing crews knew the *Endeavour* had not returned to port and they would all be on the lookout for any signs of her. Word had quickly spread through the town and the whole community waited and waited for news. The harbour normally bustled with noise and cheerful chatter but not this Thursday. Work went on normally but in a haunting silence. Nobody wanted to speculate. They'd experienced these situations before and knew full well what could be the outcome. An air of fearful anticipation hung over everyone. The waiting and not knowing was a painful process.

The school bell rang out at three o'clock for afternoon break. The children ran out into the warm June sunshine to play. Fiona, limp with the stress of events, sat quietly at her desk.

'Please Miss, there's a lady outside wants to see you', little Shona Main called to her as she suddenly burst into the room.

'Thank you, Shona. I'll come out now.'

Fiona panicked inwardly. Who had come? What was she about to learn? She felt sick. 'No, no,' she pleaded to herself, 'please don't take Bruce and Stanley from me.' Her weak legs took her out of the classroom and there at the gate she could see Isobel with Ian. Isobel waved. Fiona started to run to her but she already knew by looking at her that the news was good. Breathless she reached her.

'They're safe, they're safe! I had to let you know!'

'Thank God! Where are they? What happened?'

They've just received a radio message from Alex McKay's boat. They sighted the *Endeavour* drifting not far off the Norwegian coast. Her engines failed and that's why they couldn't contact anybody. All their power went. They're towing her back now and they should get into port in about six hours or so from now. That's all we know, but all five of them are safe.'

'Thanks for coming. I feel so much better now. What a relief! I'd really started to think they'd gone. I'll call round to see you on my way home at four.'

A huge weight lifted from Fiona immediately. She felt relief and joy overcome her. The two of them, Bruce and Stanley, would be home tonight and they were safe and well. Only minutes ago she thought they'd gone for ever. Suddenly she knew the answer! There was no doubt in her mind anymore. It was only when faced with losing Bruce did she face the truth. Of course she loved him. Of course she wanted to marry him. It was such a simple, easy decision!

That evening she was there at the harbour with Isobel as the *Endeavour* was towed in. A small crowd had gathered to greet her and her rescue ship, *Skerry*. The whole community showed its relief at their safe return.

Bruce waved to her and jumped ashore.

'Thank God you're safe! What a fright we've had. I had to come down tonight to see you. My answer's "yes" if your offer still stands,' she blurted out with relief.

'That's the best news I've had today,' he chuckled and put his arms round her and kissed her eagerly.

'Hear that, Stanley? My luck's just changed. Fee's asked to marry me at last. Do you think I should accept?' Even after all the ordeal of the previous twenty-four hours he still could joke with Stanley.

'Only if we can all go out celebrating tomorrow night. I'm too tired tonight.'

Isobel was clearly delighted. 'Well done, the two of you. We can have a double celebration tomorrow. A safe homecoming and an engagement!'

'I love you, Fee.'

'And I love you too Bruce,' she replied.

Deep down she felt at peace. She knew she'd made the right decision. Now, she'd so much to look forward to!

Printed in the United Kingdom
by Lightning Source UK Ltd.
109782UKS00001B/36